IT WAS A DEAD-END CORRIDOR

No place to hide. No place to run.

Then there was a hissing of powerful hydraulic gears behind the reinforced walls of concrete and steel, and the heavy security door slid sideways.

They rushed and jostled inside the familiar lobby leading to their quarters. Mac was last, though, turning and stabbing a finger onto the red emergency button that closed the door. After a moment's hesitation, it began to move shut, agonizingly slowly.

Jim stood near the shrinking gap, peering into the passage outside. He saw a flicker of movement and heard shouting.

A rough strident voice called out. "Hold it!"

A man appeared around the bend of the corridor, with a sawed-down scattergun cradled in his arms. "Hold the bastard door!"

The gun was leveled, barely fifty feet away.

Jim Hilton was frozen, aware that the gap was still five feet, and that an ominous grinding sound came from the door's gearing.

EARTH BLOOD

JAMES AXLER

A GOLD EAGLE BOOK FROM
WORLDWIDE®

TORONTO • NEW YORK • LONDON
AMSTERDAM • PARIS • SYDNEY • HAMBURG
STOCKHOLM • ATHENS • TOKYO • MILAN
MADRID • WARSAW • BUDAPEST • AUCKLAND

It's sometimes difficult for a father to convey to his children
the boundless extent of his love for them. His pleasure in their
company, his admiration for their individual strengths and his
respect for the way they have each coped with adversity. With
all of that, and immeasurably more, this book is for
David, Cathy and Matthew.

First edition November 1993

ISBN 0-373-63807-8

EARTHBLOOD

Copyright © 1993 by Laurence James.

"Beneath the urbane, smiling mask of polite society lies the bloody snarl of primitive murder."

—from "Yesterday's Now,"
by Gordy Newman
Privately printed, 1990

"O brave new world,
That has such people in't."

—William Shakespeare
The Tempest

1

The infinite cold and silence of the final frontier of deep space.

The exterior of the USSV *Aquila* had once been mirror smooth and diamond polished. Now it was scarred and pitted, the heat shields pocked by dust and radiation from the unknowable winds that blew between the dark stars.

The stillness beyond the locked observation shutters was continued inside the vessel.

A light film of the thinnest oil eased tumblers. On the control panels there was a dazzling array of changing colors. On the master console the micros selected from the thousands of pieces of input data.

A comp clock revealed the date and the time, the pulsing chron crystal accurate over a thousand years to one thousandth of a second.

The clock still registered Pacific coast time. It was fifteen minutes past three in the morning on the twenty-fourth day of September in the year of our Lord 2040.

A liquid-crystal display beneath was running in tandem, showing the total elapsed time of the *Aquila*'s mission.

Thirty-two seconds.

Fifteen minutes.

Twenty-one hours.

Nineteen days.

Two years.

Apart from the almost inaudible humming and whispering of the computers, the vessel was silent, the crew all sleeping.

AFTER the blast-off in the bright dawn at the rebuilt Stevenson Air Base in Nevada, the *Aquila* had been set on course for its exploratory mission. That was seven hundred and fifty days and nights ago, but the ship's crew of ten men and two women had been locked into sleep for all but twenty-six days of that time.

A form of cryonic suspended animation enabled them to be maintained at a minimal level of life support during the months of darkness, with the on-board computers, linked to those back at Stevenson, making the occasional minimal correction.

They'd all been awake on six-hour rotating shifts for the first week of the mission. Then they each entered a capsule of clear arma-glass engineered to their own body measurements. A mix of chemicals sent them sliding into something approximating sleep. Respiration and circulation both dipped to almost unbelievably low levels, levels that specialists would have interpreted as showing certain clinical death only a few years earlier.

Tubes connected to the inside of each crew member's right arm carried regular doses of balanced nutrients, while the waste products were siphoned hygienically away.

They'd all been woken when the *Aquila* was close to the halfway point of its research mission. They remained awake and busy with their various tasks for a few weeks or so and then returned, with some reluctance, to their moulded pods.

Aboard the *Aquila* there was almost no sense of time passing or of distance traversed. But the vessel was speeding inexorably back toward its home planet. Sling-shotting on its predestined orbit, back to Earth.

Eleven of the twelve crew were peacefully asleep.

One was not.

Suddenly an alarm began to shrill on board the *Aquila*.

2

Millions of dollars had been spent on researching the best sort of voice for the computer control on board *Aquila*.

It was found that people responded best to a voice that promised them security. The box most often ticked on the query-response documentation was the one that said, "A voice that promises nothing will ever happen to hurt me."

It was a female voice, within the age parameters of thirty-eight to forty-seven. Gentle and reassuring, yet with a hint of insistent strength, it was the kind of voice that a rosy-cheeked lady from Kansas City might have.

All of the astronauts called her "Mom."

This calm, motherly voice responded to the high-pitched bell, buzzer and whooping siren.

"Time to get up, boys and girls. Time to rise and shine now."

Nothing happened.

Hidden lights began to flash at the point where the *Aquila*'s ceiling and wall made their seamless kiss.

"This is not an emergency. This is automatic wakening to make preparations for reentry and landing back on Earth. Time to be up and at them, boys and girls. Rise and shineandshineandshine . . ."

There was a loud click, and the voice ceased. But the lights, bells, siren and buzzer all continued in a crescendo of noise.

Within the control units of each of the life-support capsules, there were changes made in the chemicals entering and leaving the cardiovascular systems of the astronauts.

Very gradually the state of suspended animation that had carried them through infinite miles of space was itself being suspended.

The microcharges that had prevented muscles from atrophying disconnected themselves.

Mom's voice clicked back on again. But it had suffered a subtle change. It had risen very slightly in tone, as though mildly irritated by the slugabed tardiness of her dozen recalcitrant charges.

"Wakening is proceeding. There are thirty-two hours to reentry into Earth's atmosphere and approximately thirty-six hours to the projected landing time. Wakening is proceeding."

During most of the seven hundred and fifty days and nights of the flight, the lighting aboard the *Aquila* had been very subdued. Mission control back in the Nevada desert had been monitoring everything that went on inside the vessel and making minute changes every few hours.

Now the lighting was bright again, flooding the cream-painted interior and bouncing off the array of instrumentation screens.

A couple of minor illumination fittings had malfunctioned, but it made little difference to the overall level of light.

"There will be another call in sixty minutes. Meanwhile, all other audiovisual systems will be closed down."

The ship was restored to its former silence, the twelve capsules, six to the port and six to the starboard, still slumbering.

A new clock had become illuminated, headed Time To ELT. It showed thirty-five hours and fifty-eight minutes to landing, with touchdown scheduled at Stevenson for approximately four o'clock in the afternoon of September 25.

EACH CREW MEMBER had been allowed up to sixty seconds of time to describe himself/herself for the media on a microtape that was then stored in the ship's main data base. Some had used most of their minute, while some had used a lot less.

"Hi, I'm Jim Hilton and I'm captain of the United States Space Vessel *Aquila*. I'm thirty-two years old, stand six feet two inches tall and weigh in around one-ninety, depending on how much chocolate fudge sundae I've been into recently. Been with the space project for ten years since graduating. Been married for twelve years to my high school sweetheart, Lori, who you've maybe seen on some of the afternoon family vid shows. She was the psycho killer in *Sunstrokers*. We've got twin girls, Heather and Andrea, aged eleven. I miss them a lot. And I miss our house on Tahoe Drive, a quarter mile or so from the old Hollywood sign.

Hobbies are linked to survivalist skills. I'm a fair shot with rifle or handgun. And I love my country."

James Carmel Hilton had thinning blond hair, visible through the cover on his capsule. His heart and breathing were already beginning to speed up a little, climbing back toward normal.

The next capsule along the row held a small incised plastic tag with the name of the occupant: Marcey Cortling.

"I'm Marcey Cortling and I'm number two on the *Aquila*. My personal details and my private life are just that. Personal and private."

She was twenty-nine years old and lived alone in a neat apartment on the Stevenson base, the only crew member to do so. Her father and both of her older brothers had been Air Force officers. Marcey was five feet tall and weighed one-thirty-five. Her hair was short and dark, curling a little at the nape of the neck.

One of the trivial and yet serious problems for the scientists in setting up the two-year mission had been finding a surefire way of suppressing follicular activity. Otherwise everyone would have woken up to find their pods brimming over with their own hair and beards.

The next capsule along belonged to Steve Romero. "Steve Romero. Radio honcho on this tub. Been interested in communications since I was knee-high to a beanbug. I'm thirty-seven and a skinny six feet two. I'm a vegetarian and I practice meditation. Been married but it didn't work out."

There was a hesitation in the voice. "Son called Sly who lives with ... with his mother in Aspen. She's married again. Twice more, in fact. Boy's eighteen. Wish I saw more of him. That's all, folks."

In the identical capsule to the right of Steve Romero was a shorter, paler figure whose light blue eyes were beginning to flicker as though he was going through a period of REM-induced heavy dreaming.

"Thomas. Jefferson Lee. Twenty-four. Average height and build." The records showed him at five-seven and one sixty-five. "I'm the superstar supercargo on this can. Journalist for the *West American,* who put up a big pile of dollars to get me aboard. I live on Jackson Street in San Francisco, and my hobby's battles of the Civil War. Got a sick daddy in San Luis Obispo. Hope he's pulling on through while I'm away. Absence makes his heart grow stronger."

After a pause, he continued, "Oh, and I got a steady little girl who can't wait for me to get home and show her what she likes best." The tape finished on a cackle of sniggering laughter.

"MAC. HENDERSON McGILL. Some of the squids on this jaunt call me Grandad, because I'm forty-five and the oldest crew member. Actually by the time we get home again after the big sleep it could be I really will be a grandfather. Specialty's astrophysics. Don't get much chance to use it. Machines have took us over. Got two marriages, one still running. Seven kids here and there. Wife numero uno is Jeanne. Lives on Mount Vernon Street in Boston. We get on all right, I guess. Angel...that's her real name...lives not far away in Mystic, Connecticut, with the four youngest. We get on all right, I guess." He laughed. "Hobby's keeping fit and paying alimony. Jim Hilton fancies himself with a gun. But he can't bench press half what I can. That's all I got to say, except that there's times I prefer being out in space to being stuck back here on our own sick old planet.''

MOM'S VOICE WAS ERRATIC. Every minute or so it would slow to a bass slurring, like a fat old drunk on a park bench.

"Thirty hours to reentry and thirty-four hours to projected landing. Wake up, boys and girls. You've slept long enough. Rise and shiiine. Recovery proceedings are on line and—''

There was a loud snapping sound on the tape, like a dry branch cracking under a heel. The voice went on, calm and unhurried. "There appears to be a minor malfunction with off-target reanimating proceedings. Thisthisthis investigated soonest.''

THE LAST OF THE PODS at the end of the first row held the youngest member of the *Aquila*'s crew, who also happened to be the only black on board.

Kyle Lynch was tall and slender. "Navigator. Me and Mac feel the same about our jobs.'' His voice was very quiet. "I watch a screen controlled by a preprog computer.

Anything needs changing in course or any other nav-factor input, then I still sit and watch. I'm only there for a worst-worst scenario. Triple-red days for Kyle. But if that ever happened to the *Aquila*, then I guess we'll all be chilled meat anyway. I double up as the main stills and vid photographer for the mission. Load, point and press. Ansel Adams I'm not. I live in Albuquerque down in New Mexico and I surely hope my fiancée, Leanne, is still waiting for me when I get back."

His lips moved in the stillness of the capsule as he whispered the name of his dearest love. "Rosa," he said.

TIME HADN'T meant anything to the twelve men and women on the *Aquila* for almost a year. Now it was forcing its way back into their lives.

"Twenty-nine hours to reentry and thirty-three hours to home plate. Goal line. Checkered flag. Finishing tape."

Now there was movement within the pods.

Carrie Princip, the second navigator, was a skinny blonde with long hair, aged twenty-five. Unmarried, from New Orleans.

Breathing was faster, clouding the inside of the arma-glass.

Mike Man. Quarter Chinese and the best chess player in the crew. He was a computer technician, twenty-nine years old, married with two little boys. Originally from Queens, he'd moved with his wife and family to Encino, California.

Fingers and toes began to flex and extend, and eyes opened blindly.

Bob Rogers. Single man from Topeka, aged thirty-two. The *Aquila*'s doctor, dentist and the assistant radioman.

"The life-support systems will begin to open in five minutes from now. Remember that you will all suffer some degrees of weakness. Make no hurried or sudden movements. If in need of... Push... mergency button for aid."

Pete Turner was the second pilot. Thirty-six years old, he was a widower with no children, born and raised in Omaha, Nebraska. Since his wife's death at the hands of a group of muggers on New York's Lower East Side, he'd devoted much of his spare time to becoming highly skilled in unarmed combat.

Electronics expert Jim Herne was twenty-eight and came from Vermont. He'd played pro football for the Giants as free safety until a bad knee injury finished his career.

"One hundred seconds to release. Be patient, boys and girls, before you come out to play."

Twelfth and last of the mission crew was Ryan O'Keefe. Thirty years old, the quantum-physics expert had been in charge of the most important experiments in deep space. He was also a qualified psychiatrist, specially trained in stress control and interactive interventional analysis.

Twelve men and women.

"Ten seconds to release," said Mom seductively. "Nine, eight, seven, six, five, four..."

Sunrise was beginning its sweep across the continental United States, tens of thousands of miles away from the *Aquila*.

It activated sensors all around the razor-wire perimeter of the Stevenson Air Base, switching off the lights. The endless strips of concrete, scarred with the black rubber smears of countless landings, stretched away and away toward the stillness of the gray desert.

A lone coyote trotted unhurriedly across the base, muzzle red with clotted blood.

3

There was a faint hiss of hidden hydraulic controls operating. In a ragged approximation of synchronicity, the lids of the capsules slowly began to raise themselves.

Mom's voice was positively euphoric. "Welcome back to all of you. Take care how you get up and move slowly. Remember you're still in...ficial gravity. Get some nourishment before...ming tasks. Twenty-eight hours and thirty minutes to reentry. Thirty-two hours and thirty million, billion, trillion... Correction. Thirty-two hours and thirty minutes to estimated landing."

"Shut the fuck up, Mom," sighed Jeff Thomas, giving the finger to the nearest speaker.

"I see a year's sleep hasn't done much to improve your language," said Marcey Cortling.

All around the main sleep compartment of the *Aquila,* the crew were stirring, stretching and moaning as their bodies started the process of readjustment to light and life.

Jim Hilton swung his legs over the side of his own pod, leaning his head on his hands. "Done this Sleeping Beauty act four times now, and it doesn't get any easier."

Henderson McGill laughed. "Sounds like that old joke about having sex. Woman says her husband only ever did it twice. First time he was sick, and the second time his hat blew off."

Mom came in, solicitous as a trained children's nanny. "Remember to...ake ...are. Don't make any...den movements."

Kyle Lynch was first onto his feet, grinning around him. "Mom sounds like she's gotten glitched up while we were asleep."

Hilton stood, rocking a little in the artificial four-fifths gravity of *Aquila.* "Funny that mission control didn't sort the old lady properly while we were out."

Jed Herne was the next crew member upright. "I'll try and fix it, Jim. Give me something to do on the long way home."

"Be back on base in a day and a half, Jed. Not worth it. Just switch her off, will you?"

Steve Romero uncoiled himself from his capsule, knees cracking as he straightened. He looked through to the small radio communications section. "Thought they'd have been pumping questions at us by now. The way they monitor everything they usually want to know when anyone takes a dump."

"Everyone knows when you do, Steve," teased Carrie Princip, trying to brush back her long hair, finding it was floating in a sea of static.

Pete Turner, the *Aquila*'s second pilot, was practicing some of his martial-arts kicks and punches, grunting with the effort. "I don't feel so bad." He glanced at the shadowed pod immediately behind him. "Typical of Topeka's finest. Still dead to the world. Come on, Bob!"

"Rise and shine, Bob," called Ryan O'Keefe. "Or we'll set Mom on you."

Jim Hilton was moving toward the main part of the control module. "Get Bob up, will you, Pete? He's supposed to check us all out on reanimation. Then join me in the hot seats."

"Sure, Captain Hilton, sir." Snapping off a crisp salute, Pete bent over the adjacent pod. "Get some lead in your pencil, buddy. Come on and— Oh, no. Holy shit!"

"What, dead to the world?" said Mike Man, pulling on a pair of soft-soled sneakers.

"Yeah," said Pete. "Very."

They gathered and stood around in silence, looking at the corpse, glaringly lit by the overhead strip lamps. Jed had turned down Mom's spasmodic muttering until it was just a background murmur.

Bob Rogers had been a heavily built man with a narrow black mustache. He'd worn contact lenses in his dark brown eyes.

"How long?" asked Carrie Princip, breaking the silence.

"He was the doctor. Shame we can't ask him for a postmortem."

"Not funny, Jeff." Jim Hilton shook his head. "State of the body, I'd say he's been dead for weeks. Skin like leather."

The brown eyes were gone, melted back into the cavernous sockets. The lips had shrunken and peeled off the excellent teeth. The plumpish cheeks were sunk inward, and the lower jaw gaped, accentuating the skull-like appearance. Bob Rogers's hands had turned into crooked claws, the nails digging into the hard skin of the palms.

"Weeks! Jesus, how come mission control never picked up anything wrong on their monitors and scanners?" Steve Romero turned angrily away. "Got to be some real major communications foul-up. Some gold-star asshole needs an ass kicking."

Jim Hilton looked over at his number two. "What d'you reckon, Marcey?"

She pursed her lips. "Mom's speech was screwed up, as well. Something out of the park here. Maybe we ought to contact mission control right away."

"Makes sense. Pete, you and Ryan cover him up. Just lower the capsule lid on him and seal it. Will do for the time being."

"Sure."

"And turn up the air freshener." Jeff Thomas pinched his nose.

The dead man didn't smell all that much. The various chemicals that had been pumping through him had helped suppress some of the processes of putrefaction. But there was still the distinct sour-sweet odour of decay.

"Let's get to it, ladies and gentlemen." Jim Hilton sighed. "Poor way to return. Still... Everyone to command positions, and we'll start to fly the old eagle home again."

THE WHOLE CREW were seated in their regulation deep-space flying configuration.

Jim was in the captain's chair, with Marcey at his left side, both facing forward through the vid ports. Kyle Lynch, the navigating officer, sat immediately behind Jim, and communications operator Steve Romero was jammed in next to him.

The others were sitting farther aft in *Aquila*, everyone conscious of the rotted corpse of Bob Rogers, which was hidden inside its capsule.

"Testing intercom," said Jim. "Everyone receiving me?"

There was a chorus of muttered affirmatives, all the way down the line to the supercargo journalist, Jeff Thomas.

"All right, everyone, now hear this. Bob's death's cast a giant shadow over this mission. Up to now it's gone well. We got there. We did what we had to do, and we're on the way back. Just one of those things, I guess. Seems like there was an equipment failure and he just . . . figure he just stopped breathing.''

''Still like to hear the answers to some questions from some lard-ass at control as to why it wasn't monitored and fixed,'' said McGill, his voice crackling through the quiet vessel.

Jed Herne's voice slipped in. ''Only been awake for a few minutes, but there's other things gone wrong on the electronics front, Skip, that need some thought. Looks like a failure in communications between us and Earth.''

Steve Romero heard the ball lobbing over into his section of the court. ''Meaning it's me that's fucked up, Jed?''

''No. Just looks—''

''Heard you say it was communications.''

''Yeah.''

''So that's me, right?''

Jim Hilton cut off the squabble before it deteriorated any further. ''Enough, guys. Plenty of time to sort this out after reentry. Could be that you're both right. Debriefing'll show us what went wrong, and when.''

"My intercom isn't working properly, Jim," called Jeff Thomas.

"You hear me at all?" Jim asked, channeling him through Steve so he could be patched in with the others.

"That's better. There's a lot of breakup. And the servo on my chair isn't functioning, either."

"Same with mine," added Carrie Princip. "The dupe board on the nav console is showing false data for our approach trajectory."

Ryan O'Keefe coughed apologetically. "Sorry to add my mite to the problems, but I couldn't open my personal locker when we got woken. The security device on it seemed to have jammed."

"All right, all right." Jim Hilton couldn't hide how angry he was. "Have to be breakdowns along the line. We've got a whole day to sort these things out with mission control before hot-zone time. Steve?"

"Yo, Captain."

"Let's get in touch, shall we? Establish what might have happened."

"Sure thing." He pressed and turned dials. "*Aquila* calling mission control. Come in, Stevenson. Do you read?"

Everyone on the vessel could hear the faint atmospheric hissing.

And nothing else.

4

"Twenty-seven hours and nine minutes to the commencement of final reentry procedures ... procedures." Mom lapsed into silence for thirty heartbeats. "Thirty-one hours and eight minutes to preset landing time at mission base."

The last burst of information came out at a babbling, hysteric speed, as though Mom had been secretly sniffing helium, but nobody on the crew was paying the comp voice much attention.

They'd moved back out of the control section of the *Aquila*, going through into their rest quarters. The ship had originally been designed for the crew to be split up into shifts, so that no more than three-quarters would be awake at any one time. Now, with everyone there except for Steve Romero, it was uncomfortably crowded.

The radio operator was still at his post, leaning forward, trying every channel, his voice growing hoarse with the repeated, futile efforts to raise some kind of response from Earth.

"Come in, please. This is the USSV *Aquila* broadcasting an international Mayday call. Please respond to this wavelength. Come in for the *Aquila,* homeward bound from deep space."

As they spiraled closer to Earth, Steve tried again and again. Mission control wasn't responding from Nevada. The Thatcher Memorial Research Base in Surrey was silent, and so was the Yeltsin Space Center, near what had once been called Volgograd, in the wastes of ancient Kazakhstan.

Bases in India and Australia and South America and the Arctic and Antarctic were dead and still as a nameless tomb in a desert of permafrost.

Jim had called up the ship's manuals onto the screens while all of the experts concentrated on their own areas of specialty. Section by section, everything was rapidly checked. Aerials and the outside linking receivers were all examined with the tiny mobile vid cameras.

Nobody could find anything wrong.

Steve Romero's voice flooded into the room where everyone else was huddled. "Come in, please. This is the *Aquila,* flying on down."

Jim Hilton clapped his hands. "All right, everyone. Let's just look at this one together. Anyone got any ideas?"

Nobody spoke.

"*Aquila* calling Earth. This is the USSV *Aquila* calling fucking anyone!"

Jim Hilton sighed. "So nobody's got any bright ideas?"

"Got to be something down between Earth and us," said Marcey Cortling. "Major fault that means we've totally lost all contact."

Henderson McGill shook his head. "Real brilliant, Marcey. Tell us something we don't know."

"What we don't know is everything." Michael Man was perched uncomfortably on the edge of one of the bunks.

"Sounds pretty zen," Carrie said with a smile, but it was a thin, frightened smile.

Mom's voice came through the speakers, unexpectedly loud. "We shall be commencing our descent through the atmosphere at noon on the twenty-fifth day of September. Thank you for flying Aquila Airlines."

"Having a breakdown, by the sound of it," said Pete Turner.

Mom hadn't quite finished. *"Midi, le vingt-cinq Septembre."*

"What?" Ryan O'Keefe laughed. "Now she's gone bilingual on us."

"Mittag, der fünf und zwanzigste September."

"Trilingual now."

The computer-generated voice fell silent, leaving them to consider their situation again. Steve Romero had finally given up on his Mayday calls, joining the others.

"We've got a whole day and night to check this out and establish contact with mission control." Jim Hilton stood up.

Jeff Thomas raised a hand. "What if we don't get in contact? Do we burn up on the way down?"

"Probably not, though it could get warm. The ship's programmed to get through even without help from Stevenson."

"How about landing?"

The captain rubbed fingers through his thinning, pale blond hair. "I did it often enough on the simulators. But there isn't any question of that happening, Jeff. Must be some sort of electrical interference up above the atmosphere. Once we break through, everything'll be fine and we'll be back on target again."

Jim Hilton wished that his own voice had sounded a little more convincing.

IN THE NEXT FEW HOURS the crew of the *Aquila* began to piece together a partial picture of what had been happening during the second "sleep" of the two-year mission or, put another way, what *hadn't* been happening.

It was like an infinitely complicated jigsaw puzzle with some vital sections missing or wiped clean.

Kyle found that the automatic cameras set up to record a three-hundred-and-sixty-degree view around the big shuttle every fifteen minutes had malfunctioned.

"Got pix all the way up to ten months ago. Not long after we capsuled again. Then zilch."

"Camera fault?" asked Jim Hilton, sitting in his pilot's seat and receiving the variety of status reports from everyone.

"Comp-control failure emanating from Stevenson," replied the navigator. "Most of the course-correction data ceases around the same point. Like they stopped caring about us."

Pete Turner had been recalling some of the routine input tapes received by the *Aquila* while the crew were in their state of suspended animation. Normally that would have been one of the jobs of the late Bob Rogers.

"They stop, as well, Captain. Ten months ago. Everything since then is blank."

Jim Hilton closed his eyes. "Shit," he said wearily. "Think this is some sort of exercise? One of their fun little tests?"

Mac was leaning on the back of his seat and he laughed. "Too realistic for one of their realistic simulations, isn't it?"

"Guess so. You got any ideas? You been around longer than any of us."

McGill shrugged. "Eighty years ago I'd have said the Commie bastards had come out of their tunnels and started the next . . . the *last* world war. But now . . . I really don't know. Could there be any clues on the news tapes?''

Jim Hilton called up Jed Herne. "Mac suggests a look at the most recent news input tapes in the return familiarization section of the library. Can you do that now?''

"Sure thing.''

The ex-quarterback made his way along toward the stern of the shuttle, up a narrow ladder, his old knee injury barely noticeable.

He called back to the captain almost immediately. "Tapes stop. Nothing incoming and recorded since the middle of January. Fifteenth. Usual two-minute updated bulletin. All the earlier ones are there.''

"Put it through, Jed.''

"Last one?''

"Sure.''

"Hey!''

"What is it?''

Jed sounded puzzled. "Just noticed. The tapes after January. It's not that they never came in, though . . . Oh, I get it. From January through to the beginning of April they came in on schedule, but something happened then to instigate self-erase mode. Yet there's no command record here."

Jim Hilton glanced across at his number two, raising his eyebrows. But Marcey didn't offer any kind of response.

"Yeah. After the start of April they never came in no more. Nothing. Whatever happened to freak out the comps on the ship must . . . it must've happened between the middle of January and the middle part of April."

"Put the last one on the intercom, Jed. Might be something in it."

"Sure. Here it is."

The voice was male, perfectly calm and ordinary. Jim recognized it as belonging to the broadcaster whom he'd met down at Stevenson on one of the media picnics.

"Andy Corwen," Jim said. A man who was visibly brimming with the extraordinary self-deluding self-importance of the professional, network newsreader.

"Here's the way it is for the fifteenth day of January, '24. The headline story is the fire at the Felix Turner Hospital in Shreveport, Louisiana. Latest figures put deaths at forty-two, with many more missing. Local fire chief Randall Meissen says first indications are that the fire may have suspicious origins. The Presidential primaries will shortly be opening in New Hampshire with little change in the opinion polls. The homicide of alleged Mafia hitman Larry 'Bookman' Giacomo in San Bernardino last night is believed by police to be part of an ongoing feud between warring families.''

''Can't wait to get back home to all this death and violence,'' said Marcey Cortling. ''Two years away and nothing changes.''

The taped news bulletin was continuing.

''Vid rock superstars the Mutant Scum Legion continue to break all venue records in their tour of the Bible Belt, while also outraging the Mothers of Moral Rectitude. Conference championships this coming Sunday, building toward Superbowl in San Diego in two weeks. Federal intervention has today been threatened in . . .''

''He never told us which teams are through,'' moaned Jed Herne. ''What an asshole!''

'' . . . dispute which has already lasted five months and brought the nation's capital grinding to a halt. Heavy snows are forecast across the Pacific Northwest in the next twenty-four hours. Finally an item of international news. The fundamentalist military government of Kurdistan has complained to the World National Council over alleged outrages in their border conflict with southern Iraq. There are unsubstantiated claims of chemical and ecological warfare using agrarian toxins. And that's how it is."

There was a loud, final click as the tape reached its end.

Jim Hilton looked around at the rest of the crew. "Doesn't sound like the last bulletin before the horsemen of the apocalypse come galloping in with the final curtain, does it?"

Kyle Lynch spoke for everyone. "Just sounded normal to me. No clues at all."

"Usual crap. No reason for us to get cut off up here." Ryan O'Keefe shook his head. "Nothing at all."

But they were all wrong.

5

Henderson McGill was Jim Hilton's oldest friend on the *Aquila*. They'd come through basic training in the same year, after Mac's transfer from university, and they'd both been out into deep space a number of times.

Now they sat together in the ship's small astrophysics laboratory. On the wall behind the captain the repeater clock showed that they would be coming up to reentry in less than two hours, with the projected landing back at the USAF base a little under six hours off.

The strain of the past day and night was showing on Jim Hilton's face, and he rubbed at his bloodshot eyes. "Jesus, I've had it."

"You manage any sleep?"

Jim gave him a wan smile. "Sure. I reckon I managed all of nine seconds. You?"

"I figure I must've dozed for a couple of hours during the night."

"So we head for burn-up at noon. Sounds like one of those cheapo-cheapo vid productions that Lori was always appearing in. *Burn-up at Noon.*"

McGill was rolling a blunt pencil between finger and thumb. "We had twenty-four hours to come up with an answer, Jim."

"We don't even have much of a guess, never mind anything like an answer."

The older man sniffed. "You turned me on years ago to that Victorian detective guy. You remember? Sherlock Holmes?"

"Sure. Moriarty and going over the falls. Elementary, my dear McGill. What about him?"

"He said something like, when you had a problem, after you've eliminated all the sensible possibilities, then what you've got left, however stupid, has to be the solution."

"Problem's easy as can be, Mac. Mission went well. We all go back into the sleepers. While we're out something happens. Bob Rogers goes off on the last flight west." He hesitated. "Poor bastard. Communications folded its tent into the night and stole away."

"Nice image, Jim. Should've been a poet instead of a starship commander."

"Sure. No clues. No radio response anywhere on Earth. So, logic says something has to be wrong.... I mean really very wrong, Mac, back home."

"Surely they'd have found some way to let us all know?"

"Yeah, I just... Look, talk's cheap and action costs. Best get ready for reentry. If we're going to have to take over on manual, then I guess I'd best get in some reading on the controls. Been a long old time, you know."

McGill nodded. "Sure. Remember one thing, won't you, Jim?"

"What?"

"Port is left and starboard is right."

"EVERYONE BELTED IN SAFE? I got around five minutes showing."

"Assuming the clock's working, Captain," said Marcey Cortling, "and that it won't go the way of Mom." Steve Romero had finally switched off Mom, with the help of Mike Man.

The computer control had been deteriorating with increasing speed, leading to the motherly Kansas voice gibbering out streams of numbers and abstruse mathematical formulae in high-pitched, fluting tones.

Kyle Lynch's voice came through the intercom. "Checked the data on reentry comp control, and it all looks like an ace on the line. Can't find anything wrong."

Jim Hilton laughed. "Comes under the category of famous last words, Kyle."

As the *Aquila* encountered the top surface of the atmosphere, it was beginning to vibrate. The outside sensors were already inching up the temp scale, out of the green and into the pale yellow section of the repeater dials, but still way short of the crimson segment.

"Least we might be able to get a better view of Earth once we break through." Kyle was gripping the arms of his seat with white-knuckled fists. "Cameras and deep-focus lenses all show a blur. Could be cloud cover, but you wouldn't expect the whole planet to be shrouded like that."

The shaking was building up, and the interior of the ship was filled with a piercing humming noise.

The temperature was out of the yellow and sliding fast toward orange.

"Hang on, everybody," said Jim Hilton, calm as if he were taking the twins for an afternoon drive into the Hollywood Hills. "Here we go."

6

"Jeff's puked in his lap."

"Shut your mouth, McGill, or..."

There was laughter from everyone on board as they slipped off the restraining harnesses and stood up again, all of them conscious of the control-induced increase in the ship's gravitational field.

"Or what, squid?"

The journalist was wiping at the splattered mess across the front of his dark blue coveralls. "Shouldn't have eaten two portions of that recon mush crap stew shit."

Jim stretched, rubbing the muscles at the nape of his neck. "Well, that's about as good a burn-through as I've known. Thanks a lot, mission control. You done us good."

Everyone in the crew, except for Jeff Thomas, had a precisely programmed set of tasks to do once they'd cleared reentry.

While he tried to get himself clean, the rest went to their stations.

The clock was showing three hours and eighteen minutes to estimated landing time.

ONCE AGAIN Steve Romero set about trying to establish some sort of contact with the ground crews far below them in the heart of the Nevada desert.

"*Aquila* coming home. *Aquila* coming home. Do you read?"

Jim had asked him to patch the link through the ship's intercom so everyone on board knew what was happening.

"This is USSV *Aquila* returning after two-year deep-space mission. Hello, control, can you read me? Can you read?"

As he waited, they could hear the faint hiss of clear air.

"Can't get a thing on any wavelength, Skip," he called. "I've set it to automatic search. Should pick up any broadcast. Normally it'd be going crazy by now. Thousands and fucking thousands for it to pick from. But it's going all the way up and down and finding nothing."

"You mean all channels are dead?"

Steve answered Mike Man's question. "Course not. Don't be stupid! Means we got some sort of horrendous equipment failure. And that means..."

"Means I'm going to have to bring her in with a hands-on landing," said Jim quietly.

"I'll keep trying. Could be they can hear us and we can't hear them. If they know we have a serious problem, they might be able to scramble a high-alt bomber and link something through that way. But the readings all show normal."

"Just keep on, Steve."

"Wait a minute."

"What is it, Jeff? As if I can't guess what you're goin' to say."

"Bastard right, Hilton. I want to be connected to my paper right now."

Jim sighed, looking over his shoulder at the flushed, angry face of the journalist. "I know the *West American* paid an arm and two legs for you to be with us on this mission, Jeff. Can't say I liked the idea, but our lords and masters say 'jump' and we just ask them how high. But I know you're not a stupid man. If we can't raise our own mission control, then how you figure we can get your newspaper? Right? So just keep it quiet and start thinking about the story you'll have. About being on board the first shuttle ever to come through safely with an old-fashioned pilot operating manual controls.''

It was an unusually long speech for the taciturn captain of the *Aquila,* and it even reduced Jeff Thomas to silence.

"*Aquila.* This is Alpha Quebec Uniform Indian Lima Alpha. *Aquila.* USSV *Aquila.* Anyone out there hearing us? Come in.''

There was only the hissing of the speakers, all through the vessel. Then the hissing was broken by a faint, crackling voice.

"...on...ee...een.''

"Say again. Say again. This is *Aquila.* Getting broken-up message on seventeen two five. Say again.'' Steve was fiddling with the controls, trying to strengthen the frail signal.

"What did he say?'' asked Marcey. "Anyone catch what he said?''

"Thought he said something 'me' and 'see,' and then it sounded like 'green.' But I'm not sure.'' Ryan O'Keefe shrugged. "Hell, I'm not sure.''

"*Aquila.* Say again.''

From out of the hissing the voice cleared for a minute.

"*Aquila*'s the Latin for *eagle,* ain't it? Read that some..." There was a burst of atmospheric static, followed by "...sixteen."

"Again. Try it again and give us some station identification, please. Over."

"Said that John 3:16 was what it was all about. Over."

Carrie called out. "Reference from the Bible, Captain. John's Gospel. Third chapter, sixteenth verse. Used to see banners being held up at sporting events until they stopped the religious crazies a few years back. That's what he means."

"Think he's a religious freak?" Jim pointed to Steve. "Try him again."

"Read you better now. Give identification. Who are you?"

"John 3:16. Over."

"What's the quote? You know, Carrie?"

"Funny. I looked it up once and it stuck. Something about God so loving the world that he gave his only begotten son. Who believes in him shall not perish but shall have everlasting life."

"Tell the guy we understand his reference, Steve. Ask him where he is."

"We're currently over the western part of the United States," said Kyle. "Damn near right overhead mission control. How come we can pick up this lunatic radio freak and not them?"

"*Aquila* hearing you. We know the quote. Please tell us who you are and where?"

"Jeremiah. Voice in the wilderness. Lone voice crying in the desert."

"Where, Jeremiah? Please help us. We've been away from Earth for two years. Got radio problems. Tell us, Jeremiah. Over."

Cackling laughter swooped and fell like a windblown gull. "You got a problem, mister eagle. You and..." More breaking up. "I'm out close to Barstow. You all come see me. Have a nice day. Signing off. Things to...water...get me...coyotes."

"Jeremiah! Don't break contact."

The high, reedy voice said something that they all agreed sounded like "Earthblood," and then vanished from the airwaves.

"Earthblood?" said Jim Hilton. "I don't get it. What's it mean?"

IT WAS less than ten minutes later that Carrie Princip broke away from the others and entered the forward observation chamber. The heat shields and arma-shutters had been removed from the windows, and she had an uninterrupted view of Earth.

Marcey, suddenly noticing that the other woman member of the crew was missing, followed her.

"How's the old place looking?" she called. But there was no reply. "Carrie? Carrie, are you in there? What're you doing?"

"Come in, Marcey. I was... It doesn't look right to me."

"Doesn't look right! What the shit does that mean, Carrie?"

"Earth."

Marcey squeezed forward into the cramped space, kneeling down beside the slim blond second navigator.

There was little artificial light. The room was flooded with a glow from the circular ob window that seemed to be almost filled with their home planet. The clouds that had appeared to be obscuring it had vanished, and it was now startlingly clear.

"What's wrong with it? Looks... Hey, it looks the wrong color."

"Yeah. Oceans look more or less the same. But not the—" Carrie stopped.

"The land. All the parts that should be green... they're kind of red."

"Earthblood," whispered Carrie.

7

"Yeah, yeah! For Christ's sake, stop this bastard noise!" Jim looked around at the others, fists tight with anger. "We've all seen it. And we all agree on what we've seen."

"The forests and grasslands, Captain," insisted Mike Man. "Asia and America and the heartland of Europe. All turned red."

"Maybe that has something to do with our problems, Mike, and maybe it doesn't. But will you look at the clock there. What's it say? It says that in a little over two hours I'm supposed to be bringing the *Aquila* in to land in Nevada. Now, let's get that done, then we can worry about a color change in the fucking grass. Pardon my language."

The bizarre incident of Jeremiah's splintered radio broadcast had touched every single person on board the *Aquila*.

First there'd been the ghastly discovery of Bob Rogers's death. Then the horrific number of mechanical and electrical failures that mission control should have monitored and repaired, as well as the faulty cameras and erased tapes.

Finally Jeremiah and the changed face of their home planet.

Earthblood.

The clock was showing one hour and fifty-seven minutes to landing, but the main repeater that had been revealing the total elapsed time of their mission had mysteriously gone blank.

Like generations of space shuttles, the *Aquila* hadn't really been designed to handle easily in Earth's dense atmosphere. An early-mission official had once memorably compared controlling one of them to flying an iron frying pan through an ocean of molasses.

As they orbited lower and lower, Jim Hilton was beginning to have a lot of sympathy with that man's viewpoint.

There was a tendency for the craft to yaw away as it encountered some of the high-altitude jet streams that raged across the high, thin air. The speed, miles above Earth's surface, showed up on the recording device on the control panel at well over three hundred miles per hour.

The simulator that Jim had used in training was much lighter on the responses than the real thing, particularly in the comp controls for the right and left rudder.

The artificial-horizon monitor had blinked off, having shown the ship barrel-rolling through three hundred and sixty degrees. Jim Hilton felt a little happier without it. If the weather was clear over Stevenson base, he didn't anticipate any difficulties in locating the true horizon.

The vibration that they'd all been aware of during the long reentry through the atmosphere was still there, making it hard to focus on the mass of instrumentation. The green-and-yellow numbers and the arrows and dials were in a constant state of flux.

"Movement quotient's into the top orange, Captain. Climbing."

"Thanks, Marcey. Going to have our shotgun reporter sitting in a pool of puke when we get down."

Everyone had earphones on, plugged in through the ship's intercom. They were still in the glide mode, but the time was racing toward them when Jim was going to have to fire the booming retro-rockets.

Jim's secret fear, which he hadn't mentioned even to Marcey or to Mac, was that the powerful engines would refuse ignition sequences and the *Aquila* would simply plummet tens of thousands of feet to the barren lands below them.

He'd even been doing some idle mental arithmetic, trying to figure how long it would take them from fifty thousand feet. Thirty-two feet per second acceleration. But he'd gotten confused when he tried to recall what terminal velocity was for that sort of altitude.

"How we doing for Stevenson, Kyle? Keep giving me status updates."

"On course. Difficult with you on manual. The comps don't seem to want to recognize your changes of angle and direction at all."

"Yeah."

The rear starboard vid camera had cut out on reentry, but all the others were transmitting their pictures through to the bank of screens at the head of the main cabin, repeated above the captain's head in miniature.

They were currently over the Pacific Ocean, the sea invisible through endless layers of thin cumulostratus cloud.

The vessel lurched to port and dropped vertically, as though someone had pulled the plug. Jim's hands gripped the stick to pull her back onto an even keel. Behind them he was vaguely aware of a low moaning sob coming from Jeff Thomas. He caught Marcey Cortling grinning at him from the adjacent second-officer's seat and managed a thin, tense rictus of amusement back at her.

Pete Turner was doing his usual job as captain's backup, checking the input flight data that was still available from the master consoles. "Last orbit, Skipper," he said.

"Thanks."

The *Aquila* was gradually losing altitude, dropping back toward its home planet, struggling and bucking every foot of the way. Jim was literally fighting the controls, sweat beading his forehead.

"Hold steady, you bitch!"

The clock was clicking down toward the estimated landing time. At the radio Romero was still going through the motions of trying to raise Stevenson Air Base, finding every channel was still dead. Some offered the whispering of open-line static, but the others were silent as a grave.

"Clear-air turbulence, Skip," warned Carrie Princip from her scanning radar screen. "Fifteen, twenty miles ahead."

"Terrific."

"DOESN'T TIME GO real quick when you're having fun, Jim?"

Henderson McGill was the only crew member, apart from Jim Hilton himself and Marcey Cortling, who hadn't given into the lure of the pale purple, opaque plastic sick bags.

Each sported a neatly printed label: Oral-Excretion Container. Use And Dispose.

The touchdown clock had jammed at twenty-four minutes and eighteen seconds, though the tenths of seconds still whirled around in a ceaseless cascade of blurred white numerals.

It crossed Jim Hilton's mind, as he wrestled to hold the clumsy vessel on an even keel, that the whole ship was breaking up around him. At school he remembered reading the story of the wonderful hundred-year dray that lasted without a single problem for precisely a century, and then totally disintegrated on the very next day.

Mike Man, his face like stretched parchment, called through on the intercom. "Ground clock's showing Pacific time, fifteen forty-one, Captain."

Altitude was still a little over nine and a half thousand feet.

They were close enough to see the distant jagged line of the high Sierras, the white splash of Death Valley and even pick out, very faintly, the ruler-straight lines of the freeways.

"Nothing showing up on air-traffic warnings, Skipper."

"Thanks, Carrie."

"Look at the red color daubed on the sides of the mountains to the west." Marcey pointed through the side observation window. "Should be dark green conifers there."

"I don't have the time to look. Don't even have time to breathe." He half turned so that his copilot could wipe the slick beads of perspiration away from his eyes.

"Won't get down on this approach," she said quietly. "Too high."

"Yeah. Would've been ... Whoa!"

"Got her?"

"Yeah. Wanted to go off to port all on her own. Would've been good to get down in one. At least we got plenty of fuel ... maybe too much fuel if we come down hard," he said, peering at the dials. Raising his voice so everyone would hear him clearly, he added, "Case you didn't catch all of that, we're going to do a wide, sweeping circuit. Try to lose some height and also use up more fuel. Reckon we should be touching down in around half an hour from now."

"WIND SPEED ten miles per hour. Wind direction north northeast, veering easterly, gusting to fifteen miles per hour." Carrie Princip's voice was calm, unflustered. "Cloud cover below one-tenth, high. Visibility is ten-tenths. Outside temperature now seventy-eight degrees. No precipitation. Can't see any potential problems."

Jim acknowledged the information with a curt nod. His wrists were aching from the long battle with the recalcitrant shuttle, holding her steady and on the course coordinates that Kyle Lynch was chanting out to him, with Marcey calling any variations on bearing, speed or altitude.

They were approaching this time from the southwest, heading into whatever wind there was. Without instructions from the absent ground control, Jim was simply picking up what was the main runway at Stevenson Air Base.

"This is it, guys. Once I commit, there won't be any second-guessing. We're going to be beyond broke on it."

Then there it was. The expanse of sun-baked concrete, smeared with the black rubber trails of thousands of landings, stretched ahead of the *Aquila,* perspective diminishing it to a shrinking ribbon vanishing into the desert beyond.

"Ace on the line," said Marcey. "Everything's looking good."

Altitude was seven hundred and fifty feet, the shuttle rock steady.

A light flashed on the control board. "Landing abort point in ten seconds."

"Still looking perfect, Jim."

The flashing light stopped, and a loud buzzer began to sound. Then Mom's voice made a final appearance, businesslike, brisk and insistent. "Must land. Repeat, must land. Past abort point. Vessel must now land."

THE VIBRATION WAS so bad as they came in on their final approach that Jim Hilton was finding it incredibly difficult to see anything. His whole skull was shaking, making him feel as if his brain was swilling around inside.

The instrumentation was unreadable, and he was forced into making a judgment landing, watching the strip of runway as it came swooping in below the nose of the *Aquila*.

"Can't see any sign of life, Captain." Steve Romero's voice was distorted by the juddering of the ship.

Jim couldn't have cared less at that moment. His sole intent was to hold the stubby wings level and stop the bow from digging a fiery furrow along the yellow centerline of the runway.

"Undercarriage down and locked," shouted Marcey.

Out of the corner of his eye Jim caught a flash of charred and twisted metal. A wing-tip and a silver, folded tail plane. It was on the edge of the runway, half on the scorched and blackened grass.

It was unthinkable that a wrecked fighter would have been just left there, partly obstructing the main operating runway of one of the bigger air bases in the country.

Unthinkable.

Most of the captain's mind was focused on the immediate flying problem of getting down, but a small section of Jim's mind was chilled and horrified at what was happening.

His guess put them about fifty feet up, traveling around one hundred and seventy miles per hour. Still too fast, but if he tried to drop the speed the *Aquila* could come down stern first.

He saw the pile of tangled wires and hawsers in the centre of the runway. Saw the rusting, jagged cables, clear across his landing path.

Saw them way, way too late for there to be any hope of avoidance.

Marcey spotted them at the same moment, hands starting to lift toward her face. She remembered in that fraction of a frozen second that most people's last words were believed to be expletives.

"Oh, fuck," she said.

"Hang on!"

The nose was coming down.

Ten feet up.

Five.

The speedometer was still trembling over the hundred-mile-per-hour mark.

There was a surging moment when Jim Hilton thought that the nosewheel of the *Aquila* might just clear the lethal obstruction.

But it didn't.

8

A light wind was blowing across the torn wreckage of the ship.

Arma-glass cracking and falling in tinkling shards under the pressure of the crash. Liquid dripping from a dozen places. A ruptured oil line that was oozing, thick and brown, into the scraped earth. High-octane fuel, colorless, the air shimmering around it, trickled into the gray-brown dust.

Metal groaned and settled, parts torn off and scattered back along the huge gouge in the runway, the pieces of debris trailing off into the surrounding grass and dirt. When the leading wheel had caught in the pile of discarded cables, it had tipped the shuttle over onto its blunt, heat-seared nose.

There was an eerie moaning, tiny bursts of sound, almost like someone panting with excitement during the beginnings of sexual arousal. But the cause wasn't lust. It was pain.

"My leg, my leg. Oh, sweet Jesus, help me, help... My leg."

The voice so thin and strained that it wasn't even possible to work out whether it came from a man or a woman.

Jim Hilton lay still and took long, slow breaths, fighting for self-control, knowing that they'd crashed. Lost it in the biggest way. He remembered the control panel rising toward him, and the bow window starring into a million diamonds before the dust had flooded into his mouth and nose and eyes.

Now it was amazingly quiet.

"Check yourself first." Jim was certain that his lips had moved, but he wasn't able to hear any words come out of them.

Toes and feet and legs all seemed to be in place and functioning. Fingers and arms. Neck was very stiff with what felt a bit like a highway whiplash reaction. The restraining belts that crisscrossed his chest were still holding Jim in his seat, though he was hanging at a slightly crooked angle, head to one side, eyes tightly shut.

The voice behind him had fallen silent.

Finally he plucked up his courage and opened his eyes. The shuttle had cartwheeled along, shedding wings and tail plane as it did so. The remains had overtaken the fuselage and were scattered all around the nose, some of them glinting in the late-afternoon sunlight. Fresh air was coming in through the windows, every one of which was smashed.

There was a strong smell of fuel.

"Oh, no... Better move. Marcey," he called, turning to his copilot.

She was still sitting in her seat...most of her was still sitting in the seat.

The enormous strain of the crash had burst the buckles on her restraints, so that she'd been tossed to one side. Her right arm had been caught in a window and torn apart at the elbow. Her left leg had snapped in mid thigh, and the two jagged ends of the femur were protruding through the bloodied cloth of her pants.

And her head was missing.

"Oh, Christ, Marcey...."

The front of the cabin was awash with thick arterial blood, splashed everywhere, including all over his uniform.

"Skip?"

"That you, Jed?"

"Yeah."

"How is it?"

"Bad. I think I've sprained my ankle. Cut on the side of my head. Ribs bruised. Ligament strain in my injured knee."

"The others?"

"Reckon Mike Man's bought the farm. Looks as though his neck snapped. Hanging over, the back of his head sort of dangling between his shoulders. Looks kind of..."

"The others, Jed?" Jim was trying to loosen the buckle on his own seat belt with fingers that were slick with Marcey's blood. Around his groin and thighs was a sensation of cooling wetness where he'd lost control of his bladder.

"Can't see. You all right?"

"Yeah. Seem to be."

"Marcey?"

"No."

A short silence. "Can just see Ryan. Doesn't look too good. He was moaning about his leg. Now he's gone quiet."

"Carrie and Steve. Pete. Mac and Kyle? How about them?"

Jed sighed. "Can't see from where I am, Jim. Place is just smashed up to shit back here. Best come take a look."

A muffled voice reached them.

"I'm here."

"Mac?"

"Yeah. Got a seat on my head. Think it's Carrie in it. Most times I'd have jumped at the chance to have her sit on my face. Now I'd like her moved off." After a pause came the sounds of a struggle. "There. Strong smell of fuel back here, Jimbo."

"On my way."

Glass crunched under his boots as he moved. Jim had to lean on the arm of Marcey's seat to lever himself up, and he nearly vomited at the sticky warmth of the pooled blood. The *Aquila* was tilted to port, and as he looked aft Jim realized how lucky it was that any of them had survived the crash.

At least he and Jed and Mac were alive and relatively uninjured.

As he stood there, resting his hand on the edge of the control-cabin door, Jim could see a tangle of limbs. Several of the seats looked as if they had come away from their moorings and been thrown, with their occupants, toward the rear of the vessel.

Steve had blood coming from his eyes, eyes fluttering as he started to come around.

"Can you read ... read me ... ?" he muttered.

Jim stooped and checked the pulse, finding it slow but regular.

"There's a leak from the tanks, Steve. Got to get up. Now."

"Yeah, sure. Get up. On my way. Read you, Jim. Ready or not, here I come."

With a hand under the arm, the radio operator was heaved upright, where he stood swaying, looking around at the destruction.

"You all right?"

"Been better."

"Get the lock opened. Some of the others need help."

"Boy, heavy landing, Jim."

"Tell you later."

Farther back he saw McGill supporting Jed Herne. Beyond them he saw Mike Man, unmistakably dead, his neck broken by the impact of the crash.

Pete Turner was moaning softly on the floor of the cabin, doubled over in the fetal position, hands clasped between his thighs.

Carrie was still in her seat, unconscious, a large bruise across her forehead, blood trickling from nose and mouth and ears.

Oddly there didn't seem to be any sign of either Kyle Lynch or Jeff Thomas. Jim looked around the shambles, seeing piles of equipment in one corner. A foot was sticking out from under it.

"I need some help," he called, blinking at a sudden wave of dizziness.

"Door's open," shouted Steve Romero. "Big lake of fuel all around us, Jim."

"Stay out and get clear. See if there's any help on the way."

He knew there wouldn't be.

It was an extraordinary circumstance, a space shuttle coming in to land on its own at Stevenson. Ordinarily, with any threat of a crash landing, there would be a huge carpet of foam and fire trucks and blood wagons, sirens and the anthill look of organized panic.

But the base was still and silent.

"Jed's knee's not good," said Mac, framed in the aft hatch. "Best he gets out of the way."

"Let's get at it, then."

The pile of chairs and desks and computer gear in the corner suddenly began to move.

"Get this shit off of me. I'll sue for fuckin' billions for this. Oh, my face!" The voice was rising hysterically. "I'm cut! For Christ's sake, I've been fucking cut!"

"Jeff's alive," said Jim Hilton flatly.

"So's Carrie. Knocked out clean. I'll get her out in the open. The others can take her then."

McGill unstrapped the young woman and lifted her with effortless ease, carrying her like a baby toward the open lock.

"Where the fuck is everyone?" Jeff Thomas's voice was, not surprisingly, on the ragged edge of panic. "I'm bleeding here."

"Keep still, Jeff! We'll get you out in a couple of seconds."

Jim was trying to keep a count in his head, but the names and faces kept slipping treacherously away from him.

Marcey was dead. Decapitated in the crash. Mike Man was gone. Bob Rogers had died in...no, he'd been dead for a long time.

Jed and Steve were outside safe. So was Carrie. Jeff was alive.

"Me and Mac are here," Jim said to himself.

"Sure we're here, good buddy," said Mac, returning from the door.

Three dead in the ship. Maybe more. Three safe outside. Him and Mac. That made eight. Pete Turner breathing, but on the floor looking a lot less than well. Nine. Jeff Thomas made ten.

"Kyle and Ryan unaccounted for," he said to Mac.

"Ryan's gone. Right at the back, behind Mike's seat. Thrown about and got a leg caught. Ripped him open at the groin. Artery popped and he bled to death."

"Oh, shit." Jim pressed the tips of his fingers to his forehead, fighting for control. "There was a mass of wires and rope and stuff across the runway. Couldn't see it until..."

Mac patted him on the shoulder. "Later'll do for that, Captain," he said quietly.

"Let's get the others away before something shorts out and we all get microwaved."

"Get Pete out. I'll clear all this stuff away from Jeff."

Mac pointed at the foot that was sticking out from the wreckage. The pants leg above the ankle was torn, showing black skin. "Kyle's under there, as well. I'll take Pete out and come back."

"Yeah."

Now the sum added up. Four outside. Four inside, definitely chilled meat. Him and Mac. Now Kyle and Jeff Thomas.

The journalist was keeping up a frightened tirade. "For Christ's... I can smell fuel. Burning. Fuckin' move it, will you?"

A durasteel table had been ripped away from the massive impact of the crash landing and was now wedged across the corner of the cabin, pinning down everything underneath it.

Jim braced himself against the wall and kicked at one of the buckled legs, jarring it free.

"Careful, you prick! That hurt my ribs."

"Shut it, Jeff. I'm getting you out."

The panic diminished in the voice. "Sure, sure, Jim."

The captain heaved and pulled at the tangle of equipment. Without his noticing it, Mac had come back again and started using his enormous strength to rip and tear the pile apart, finally revealing Jeff Thomas, flat on his back, glaring up at them.

His nose was smashed, purple and bloody, and there was a deep cut sliced from the corner of his right eye down to the swollen mouth. His neck and shoulders were slobbered with bright crimson blood.

"Get me up, guys," he said, reaching a hand to them.

Now they could also see part of Kyle Lynch's body, motionless on its side, head right in the corner of the cabin.

"I'll take him out, Jim. Be right back."

"Sure."

Jeff doubled over as Mac helped him, none too gently, to his feet. "Oh, think I got broken ribs, as well." He looked around him at the utter devastation. "Where's everyone?"

Mac was tugging him toward the open door. "Some didn't make it. Come on, Jeff."

"Didn't make it? You mean they're dead, Mac? Who's dead? I have to..."

The voice faded, and Jim was left alone with the four corpses and Kyle Lynch.

The tall, slender radio operator was breathing, and the pulse in his throat was beating strongly. His eyes were closed, and there was a thread of blood from his open mouth.

"Kyle. Time to move, son. Journey's over and we've come home."

He shook him gently, then harder. The young man's head lolled on his shoulder, tongue protruding, drops of crimson dribbling from it.

"Here. I'll take his feet, Jim. You hold his shoulders."

Behind McGill one of the navigation computers exploded in a burst of fire and fountaining yellow-and-silver sparks.

"Barbecue'll start real soon, Jim," warned the big man.

The smell of the high-octane rocket fuel was even stronger outside the entrance to the *Aquila*. The two officers waded through the lake of volatile liquid, ankle deep in the furrowed crater created by the vessel.

Jim Hilton felt sick, his guts churning with bile. His head was spinning, and he staggered in the unaccustomed gravity of Earth.

He could dimly see the little group of survivors, sitting and standing together a couple of hundred yards away.

"Keep going," urged McGill, taking most of the weight of the unconscious man.

"Want a hand?" yelled Jed Herne.

"No! Stay there." Jim's throat hurt, and the muscles in his thighs and shoulders were fast turning into jelly.

"Want to go back for the bodies?" panted Henderson McGill. Despite his great strength, the astrophysicist was struggling to keep going.

"Rest up some. Then get them. We're nearly there."

They reached the others and laid Kyle in the dusty grass.

At the same moment the wreckage of the *Aquila* exploded in a huge ball of fire and yellow smoke, the force of the blast sending Jim to his knees, his lungs sucking in the wave of intense heat.

"Mission over," said Steve Romero.

9

The sun was low in the western horizon, beginning to set behind the Sierras. Shadows speared across the flat expanse of the Air Force base. Like a great black fist, the column of oily smoke from the burned-out wreckage of the *Aquila* punched into the cloudless sky, casting its own pall over the desert.

Jim Hilton sat in the dry dust, knees drawn up, staring blankly at the devastation of his command. He coughed, aware of a stabbing pain in his chest.

"You got something on the shoulder of your jacket," said Steve Romero. "What is it?"

Jim wriggled his arm around to peer at himself and saw a thick, clotted smear of pinkish gray, like spilled food.

"Marcey's brains," he said.

A coyote howled somewhere near the western perimeter of the airfield. Everyone turned to look in that direction.

Jed shaded his eyes with his hand. "Reckon part of the main perimeter sec fence is down. Or is it my eyes?"

Jim struggled to focus across the sand and stubbled grass. It did look as though at least three of the metal support towers were down. He also noticed something else.

He picked a few blades of grass from where he was sitting, lifted them in the palm of his right hand and peered at them.

"What d'you make of that, Mac?" he asked, offering them across to Henderson McGill.

"Grass."

"What color?"

"Green. What else?" He lowered his head. "Well, a kind of pinkish gray-green with that sandy dirt all over it."

"No. It's more red than any other color."

"Like the forests," exclaimed Carrie Princip, who was lying on her back, her head in Jed Herne's lap. "Earthblood."

The coyote gave its hunting cry again, and she shuddered.

Jim sighed. "Look. Something's wrong as it can be. We got four dead friends burned up over there. It'll soon be dark, and we need to be in the main mission command buildings by then."

They'd come to their grinding halt at the far northwest of the base, with the rectangular block of control buildings behind them—at least four miles away across two runways.

"Want a status report on everyone, Captain?" asked Pete Turner.

"Good idea. I'll start with me. I feel sick. Tired. Whiplash in the neck. But not so bad. How 'bout you, Pete?"

"Something hit me in the balls like a kicking mule. Pissing blood but it'll pass. Feel sick. I can walk, though."

"Mac?"

"Burn on the inside of my left arm. Can't remember getting it. Feel as though I've taken part in a double triathlon. Nothing that a hot bath and forty-eight hours' sleep—and a decent meal and drink—won't cure."

"Jed?"

The former pro footballer sniffed, touching his knee. "Ligament strain. Not so bad as I thought at first. Ribs sore, real sore. Ankle is strained. Not a sprain like I thought at first. Tendon pain in the left wrist. Small cut above the right ear, but it stopped bleeding. Think that's all."

Jim Hilton managed a smile. Every professional sportsman or woman that he'd ever known had been utterly preoccupied with his or her own body and its various minuscule malfunctions.

"Can you walk?"

"Guess so, but not too far and not too fast. If we're going to make the HQ by dark, I'd better get going right away." He stood up, hopping on his good leg. "Anyone noticed some of those buildings look fire damaged? Soot around doors, windows and over the roof." He hesitated. "But...but it's hard to be sure at that distance. Might be shadows."

"We'll check it when we get there." Jim turned to Carrie, who was still lying down. "How about you?"

"Just my head. Like it's been filled with Crazeefoam and helium. Reckon I can make it. Like Jed said. Slow and easy."

Jeff Thomas had been walking in small circles, kicking up puffs of dust from his expensive trainers. "Don't bother asking, Captain Hilton. You can see, can't you? If I look one quarter as bad as I feel, then your ass is history."

McGill laughed despite the bizarre horror of their situation, managing to sound genuinely amused. "Truth is, Jeff, that you look twenty times worse than you feel."

"Yeah, and fuck you, too, you..." he snarled, then stopped as McGill turned to smile at him.

"Steve?" Jim glanced across to where the radio operator was sitting in the dirt, head slumped. "Hey, Steve?"

"I'm in charge of communications, Captain. Yeah, I am." Steve was nodding wisely. "In charge, all right. Me and Jeremiah. This is Sierra Tango Echo Victor Echo signing off."

"Concussion," said Mac, shaking his head. "He'll be all right after a rest."

"I'm fine, Captain. Get them in the third quarter. Quarter as good as he feels. I just want to Papa Uniform Kilo Echo—puke, that is."

And he did.

That left Kyle Lynch.

He was barely conscious, drifting in and out, but they hadn't been able to find a single wound or injury on him, apart from his having bitten through the very tip of his tongue.

Jim knelt by him, conscious of stiffness in his knees. "Kyle. You hear me, son?"

"Tell Rosa I love her."

"You mean Leanne, Kyle. That's the name of your girl."

There was no reply.

"Concussion, as well, I reckon." Mac looked down at the skinny black man. "Least he shouldn't be too heavy to carry."

The coyote howled a third time, answered by several more of a hunting pack. The mournful calls came from the southern perimeter of the base, close by the California state line.

"Got to be two hours to reach headquarters, what with the crips and the unconscious," said Mac. "And I'm not that hopeful about what we might find when we get there."

The fire from the *Aquila* was already dying down, the pall of smoke beginning to dissipate toward the south. Slowly the eight survivors from the crash began to make their way toward the distant huddle of buildings.

The sun was now well down, and the temperature was dropping quickly. The reasonably able took turns helping the more seriously injured.

They'd gone about half the distance when they came across the first of the bodies.

10

The desert winds had desiccated the corpse, leaving it as dried-up as an Egyptian mummy. The eyes would have been first to go, along with all of the soft tissues of the face. Scavengers, probably including the coyotes, had also gotten at it, ripping open the abdominal cavity.

The bare bones of the skull shone through the taut, torn remnants of the dark skin. Teeth glittered in the twilight's last gleaming.

"Security guard," said Jim Hilton as they stood around the body.

The body was clad in the ragged remains of an olive green uniform. There was a belt around his shrunken waist and an open holster on the right hip. The tatters of hair clinging to the smooth skull were bleached the colour of straw.

Name patch on the left breast, the stitches pulled loose so that it flapped in the light evening breeze, identified the man as K. DeForrest in faded red letters.

"Anyone know him? Remember him?" McGill stooped and dipped his hand into the pockets of the uniform, but someone had been there before and they were all empty.

Nobody answered.

"How'd he die?" asked Jed Herne.

There was still enough light for Pete to point with his toe at the corpse's chest. "Shot," he said flatly. "Three times."

The white of splintered bones showed through the jagged holes.

"Could it've been a rebellion? You know, like a kind of civil war?"

Carrie Princip's halting question hung in the air unanswered.

"Might be something to do with this red grass. Everything around seems dead or dying." Jed looked at the others. "And the forests gone to blood. Like the crazy said on the radio."

"Let's keep moving." Jim led the way, away from the corpse and across the flattened, dusty land, toward Stevenson's main buildings.

When they got closer to the center of the base, they came across five or six more corpses though it could have been four or even seven or eight.

This time the coyotes had done a better job gnawing the bodies and tearing them apart. The light was almost totally gone, apart from a deep maroon glow behind the western mountains, which made it extremely difficult to check the details of the dead.

"This is more recent." Mac was stooping over one of the bodies. "Not so rotted. No uniform, just jeans, sweatshirt and working boots, badly worn. Rest look like they were shot, but this one's had his throat slit from ear to ear."

"Terrorists," said Jeff Thomas, his voice muffled and distorted by his badly broken nose. Since leaving the scene of the crash landing, the journalist had hardly spoken to the others. He'd been unresponsive, reluctant to take his share in helping Kyle and Jed Herne along.

"Terrorists!" Mac laughed, making a snorting sound in the darkness. "What kind of shit is that?"

"Lefties or righties. Some kind of guerrilla gang attacked the base. Broke the fences, smashed up some planes, set fires . . . killed the guards."

Pete Turner joined Henderson McGill in laughing at Jeff's idea. "Not just your nose got pulped, brother, your brain, too? Terrorist gang attacking one of the most heavily armed and sec defended places on the whole bastard planet!"

"Think the government wouldn't have sent along a few reinforcements, Jeff?" Mac shook his head wearily. "What went down here mostly went down months ago. Months."

"HOLD IT A MINUTE." Jim raised a hand, halting the stumbling procession. Several of the survivors immediately slumped, groaning, to the dirt, completely exhausted.

They were about a hundred and fifty yards away from the nearest of the buildings, what was once radar control, he remembered. A sickle moon had risen and was giving enough silvery light to see a little of their surroundings.

Jed's earlier observation from a distance proved accurate. Most of the deep-set windows had gone, as had the doors, and there were the charcoal smudges of smoke all around the white walls.

"Anyone see any sign of life? Fires? Lamps? Movement?"

He could answer his own question. In the clear desert air, the pillar of flame and the explosion when the *Aquila* had come down would have been visible for at least fifty miles around. If anyone was waiting for them, they'd had three hours to get their ambush prepared.

The base was still and silent and dark as a raven's wing.

"Whoever cut that poor devil's neck wide open might still be around," said Henderson.

"Thanks." Jim sighed. "Truth is, we have to get some place to lie down before we all just fall down. I figure we should head for our old quarters. Least we know that part of the base better than any other. Any other ideas?"

"Since I am radio operator, I suggest that we radio for some sleep. *Aquila* calling Sierra Lima Echo Echo Papa."

"Sure thing, Steve." Turning to face the others, Jim said, "I'm going ahead. Pete, you come with me. Rest of you, stay with Mac and keep together. I'll call if it's safe."

"What are you going to do if it's not safe, Skipper?" asked Carrie.

"I'll be the blur moving west, heading for the long swim to China."

It wasn't much of a joke, but it got a murmur of amusement from some of them.

"JESUS, CAPTAIN..." Pete Turner leaned against a scorched wall, his face a white blur in the semidarkness. "I mean...how could this...?"

"Still don't know. Guess we'll find out eventually, but till then..." Jim Hilton's words also drifted away into the echoing silence around them.

"This is real, isn't it?"

"What?"

The thirty-six-year-old second pilot hesitated. "When my Janey got butchered by those bastards on the Lower East Side...

Seems a lifetime ago. When that happened I nearly went crazy. Came home one night to our apartment, our empty apartment. Went in the kitchen and I trashed everything. Smashed every plate and cup and glass. Wrecked it, then sat in the middle and cried, Jim, cried.''

"I know, Pete. You put all this on your audio file when you enlisted in the program."

"Sure, but the point is, Jim, I nearly went crazy. Ape-shit wild. I keep thinking this is some sort of drugged dream, that I'm still safe in the pod up on *Aquila* and we're all alive and sleeping. Know what I mean?"

Hilton nodded. "Sure, I know. Like a horror vid where the world's changed all around you. This isn't a dream, Pete—not unless we all got the same dream. I got Marcey's blood on me. Your balls hurt. Kyle's concussed. Bob's dead. Ryan. Mike's body was burned up. No, it's real."

"Where'd they all go?"

"Later, Pete, later. What matters right this moment is we're all dead on our feet. Base is deserted. Go call the others up here, and we'll find some place to rest."

THERE WAS NO LIGHT, no power or heat, no way of making a fire.

"You're the survivalist, Jim," said Mc-Gill. "Can't you rub two dry sticks together, or some kinda shit like that?"

They'd not gone far into the complex and stopped to take stock.

Every man and woman in the crew was highly capable and intelligent. All of them, with the single notable exception of Jeff Thomas, had a clutch of degrees, mainly in the sciences. It would have been hard to have found a more skeptical and unsuperstitious group anywhere in the country.

Yet none of them was prepared to go wandering any deeper into the maze of linked rooms and corridors. Not in the darkness of night, with the feeling of death all around them.

The main entrance had functioned as a large lobby, glass doored, with bright murals of space travel on the walls and an inviting oasis of potted plants and comfortable seats. An information desk and a small, discreet security section had been housed in the lobby, and banks of elevators and passages gave access to other wings and floors.

It had been the surface glitz on the whole of the space-research mission, but now it was a shambles of broken glass and smashed and burned furniture, stinking of urine and old death. It was a dry and bitter stench that seemed to ooze outward from the other sections of the base.

"Let's stay here," Jeff Thomas suggested sullenly.

"Yeah. Explore when it gets light," agreed Pete Turner.

Jim was too tired to argue. He knew that they should do something about their own safety at least, find a door that would shut, and keep a watch for any threat coming out of the ranging desert.

Mac was the only one trying to make a case for more care and security.

"Who shot the guards? Who opened up that man's throat for him? We don't know. Don't know who and don't know when. Or where the killers are."

"Anyone wants to cut my throat...I'll hold still for them." Kyle Lynch had been recovering in the past hour or so and was now able to stand unaided.

"Yeah, me, too." Carrie had swept a patch of dusty carpet clear of most of the broken glass and was stretching out on it.

Mac peered toward where Jim stood in the doorway. "You're captain. What d'you say?"

"I was captain of the *Aquila,* Mac. That was then. This is now. Let's try and get something organized in the morning. Sleep'll do us all good."

That was it. They couldn't be budged for the time being. They abandoned their battered bodies to mindless, healing rest. And the most important thing that happened in the night was that nothing happened in the night.

11

Jim was dreaming.

During the twelve years of marriage he'd got used to seeing his wife in a variety of small TV or vid roles. Every now and again she'd get a break and she'd get some publicity. *Sunstrokers* was probably her biggest role, if not exactly the best.

In his dream Jim was watching a film with his two girls, Andrea and Heather, out on the patio of their sunbaked Hollywood home. The water of the pool glittered with a bland beauty, and far below, near the reservoir, a lone coyote howled.

In the film they were watching, Lori Hilton was playing one of her airhead-blond killer roles. She had two daughters, a little like Andrea and Heather, and she had murdered them both. Gutted them with a ceremonial samurai sword, throwing the bodies into the pool of her home.

Jim had gone into the cool of the house, letting himself in through the screen of the sliding glass doors. He ambled over to the bar and poured himself a vodka and Coke.

"How's the movie, girls?" he called as he walked back, blinking in the bright sunlight.

But their orange-and-chrome loungers were both empty, and the television showed only a black-and-white field of crackling static.

"Where are you?" His voice sounded muffled and flat, as if he was in a concrete bunker instead of the smoggy California air.

"Jeremiah says look for the still waters," said a sharp, maniac voice from the television.

"The pool," Jim whispered.

The girls were in the pool.

He remembered he'd once seen an exhibition of paintings from some old English guy, from the late eighties and nineties. A lot of them were lyrical pastels of California swimming pools, in idyllic blues and greens.

There hadn't been a lot of red in them.

But his pool was flooded with crimson. An opaque veil that spread upward from something near the bottom obscured the details.

He heard steps behind him. The clicking of high-heeled sandals on the tiled surround of the sunbaked patio.

"Now you, Jim," said his wife, smiling.

HIS THROAT FELT RAGGED, and he had the certainty that he must have been screaming at the top of his voice.

But when he looked around the lobby of the mission-control section of the Stevenson Air Base, Nevada, the other survivors seemed to be still fast asleep, undisturbed.

There was a strange, opalesque light filtering through the shattered frames of the entrance doors, casting uncertain shadows across the room, highlighting the thousands of shards of splintered glass on the dusty carpet.

Everyone was still there, sprawled out, heads pillowed on arms. It was like a scene from a vid—the airport lounge filled with exhausted refugees from some military rebellion.

Jim Hilton stood up, his body registering a mass of aches and pains, the muscles in legs and neck and back protesting at being disturbed. He stretched, the bloody specters of his nightmare drifting reluctantly from his mind.

Carrie Princip opened an eye, squinting up at him. "One order of eggs over easy. And the biggest pile of hash browns in the entire Western Hemisphere, please, Captain."

"I'd settle for a good big mug of fresh-brewed java," he replied.

"Yeah," she said quietly. "That, too."

"I'm going to look around some. Want to come along, Carrie?"

"Why not. Had all the sleep I'm likely to get. My head feels a whole lot better."

She joined him by the doors, her boots crunching softly.

"Looks just like always," he said. "Wouldn't know there was anything wrong."

The pinkish gold light from the early eastern dawn spilled across the entire base, touching the far-off peaks with its brightness. Jim could just make out the dark shape of the *Aquila*'s wreckage beyond the main runway toward where the field ended and the desert began.

He sucked in several long, deep breaths of the morning's freshness, feeling it sweep away the night's cobwebs.

"Tastes good after two years of recycled air that eleven other people have been breathing. Like a fine white wine."

"I promised myself that I'd line up six of the biggest and best mint juleps at a little bar I know in New Orleans, back of Ursulines Avenue. Then sit there and listen to some good music and drink them real slow, one after the other." Her voice was dreamy. "Then I figured I'd call up a guy I know. Intelligence of a fence post, but great in the sack. Spend the whole night getting laid." She shrugged, her eyes fixed on the horizon. "But now . . ."

"Yeah . . . now."

Far away to their right, toward the north, Jim could see a tiny cloud of dust, no larger than a man's fist. He stared at it, trying to figure out what it was. But it was so far off he couldn't see a thing, couldn't even see if it was moving in any particular direction. He decided it might be one of the small herds of wild mustangs that still lived and foraged up in the foothills.

"Shall we wake the others?"

He nodded. "Guess so. Reckon we should try and stick together."

"Jim?" she called, catching at his sleeve as he started to move off.

"What?"

"Where do we go next?"

The question caught him off-balance. "I haven't thought any further than right now, right this moment. I suppose I was sort of certain we'd be brought in and the cameras and press and then the debriefing, weeks and weeks of it. Then start training for the next one down the line. Oh, and see our folks, I guess. That goes without saying."

She smiled. "Least you got folks to go and see, Jim."

"Your parents...they're both dead, aren't they, Carrie?"

"Jackknifed semi near Yellowstone. Two years ago. They were on a big vacation to celebrate their silver wedding. Their second day into it."

There was movement behind them, the sound of someone coughing and quiet voices.

Jim touched the woman on the shoulder. "Look, if you'd like to come back home with me..."

"D'you think we all got homes to go to, Skip?"

"That's what most of us are going to want to find out, I suppose. Let's go see the others."

EVERYONE FELT a little better, except Jeff Thomas, who was already complaining bitterly about the pain from his smashed nose.

Both Kyle and Steve were pretty well out of their concussions.

The main problem for them all was one of general fatigue, and a spillage of the clinical aftershock from the crash and the horrific deaths of four old and trusted friends.

Jim stood in the lobby and clapped his hands, catching everyone's attention.

"First things first. Check out the base. Get to our own quarters and see if there's anything left or any messages for us...clues to what's gone down while we were away. Then..."

"Then what?" asked Mac. "If nobody objects...or got a better idea, I'd kind of like to get off east and see my wives and my kids."

"Sure." Jim looked around. "We probably all feel that. Normally our folks would've been here for the landing. They all knew the time and day. Just another storm cloud that there's not a single soul here to greet us."

"Anyone noticed the walls?" said Pete Turner. "Now that it's light . . ."

The lobby had been decorated with bright paintings, but they were all pitted and chipped with dozens and dozens of holes.

"Bullets," said Jim.

"My guess, too." The second pilot pointed through a half-open door, into the heart of the section of the base. "Went there for a leak in the night. Stumbled over something." He paused. "Someone. No, more than one. Been a hell of a firefight here, Captain. There are dead outside and more in here."

"Then we stick together."

They came across the bodies of five of Stevenson's highly trained security guards. The corpses had been mangled by predators, but there was enough left to see that they'd all been shot to death.

Jim knelt and examined the remains. "Looks like high-velocity hunting rifles. And all their weapons are gone."

"I'm telling you," insisted Jeff Thomas. "Leftist guerrillas. Took over the whole country."

This time nobody tried to contradict him.

12

By the time they reached the core of the mission-control area, they'd found eighteen dead males and three dead females.

All but one were from Stevenson. The exception was a skinny woman in a thermal vest, working jeans and high-laced combat boots. She'd been gut shot and looked as if it might have taken her a painful time to make the long day's journey into night.

The survivors of the *Aquila* only recognized the name tag of one of the dead.

"F. Thursby."

Thursby, a small man who'd had special responsibility for internal security, had been hit in the legs and then finished off with a single round through the back of the skull, blowing most of his face onto the floor.

"Poor old Floyd," said Steve Romero. "Played a mean game of pool."

All the bodies that they found within the complex looked as if they'd been dead for weeks, probably for months.

Apart from the corpses, there wasn't much to see in the base. It had been utterly stripped and destroyed. Fires had been started in several places, some of which had smoldered harmlessly, while others had ravaged whole suites of rooms and offices.

Mission-control headquarters was one of the sections that had been totally destroyed by arson. The rows and rows of desks and comp consoles were fused into ugly tangles of blackened plastic and steel.

"Nothing here," said Kyle.

"Nothing fucking anywhere," snapped Jeff Thomas. "Nobody and nothing."

Jed Herne picked up an overturned chair and sat down in it, rubbing at his knee. "No point going any farther, is there, Skipper? Just be a lot more of the same."

"Our quarters. They had arma-steel security doors. So did the armory."

"Why do we want the armory?" asked Pete Turner. "Sorry, that's a dumb-fuck question, isn't it? Sure. It was right next to the main stores area and our section."

The stores had been sucked clean. Anything that could conceivably be eaten or drunk or worn was gone, swept away as though a voracious hurricane had howled through the long underground warehouses.

"Must've been a lot of folks to clear this much stuff away." McGill sniffed. "Like a plague of locusts going through it. Mighty big gang of terrorists, wasn't it, Jeff?"

But as they moved along, the journalist ignored him.

When they got to the last gloomy length of corridor leading to what had been their private quarters, Kyle Lynch reached out and flicked on a switch. To everyone's surprise, a row of lights stuttered on, the neon buzzing in the ceiling.

"Nuke generator's still working someplace," said Mac.

There were more bullet scars in the curving walls, a perfect handprint, in blackened blood, and five more dead guards.

"It was a massacre," said Steve. "Why didn't they bring reinforcements to come and stop all this?"

"Busy somewhere else?" offered Jim.

The bend in the passage, beyond the group of corpses, finally revealed the massive security doors. The dark gray paint was chipped and gouged, showing the brightness of raw metal. A fire had been lit at the base, blackening the entrance and the ceiling above. But the doors still seemed solidly closed.

"They never got in," said Jeff. "Sons of bitches never made it."

"Didn't have the kind of high ex they'd have needed." Mac shook his head. "If they couldn't, then I guess we can't either. Unless..." He let his words trail off, looking to the right where a discreet box, less than a foot square, was fixed to the wall. "Unless they smashed the controls."

Kyle was nearest and he lifted the lid, revealing rows of small, recessed buttons, each carrying a letter or a number. "Still here."

"Anyone recall the code?" asked Mac.

The silence stretched on and on.

Steve giggled nervously. "I could never remember it. Not even when I used it ten times every day. It was four numbers and letters. Not a lot of help, is it?"

Jim shook his head. "After two years they'll have changed it a mess of times."

"If you got it wrong four times in a row, the alarm went off and everyone came running. And it brought down a permanent lock," Carrie said with a grin. "Remember when Bob Rogers got tanked up and couldn't hit the right buttons? Knew the code, but his coordination let him down."

Jim rubbed the back of his neck where the whiplash was still painful. He knew he should be showing powers of leadership. That was his job. Captain of the *Aquila*. But his brain seemed to be plowing through endless layers of oatmeal.

"Odds are millions to one against hitting the right combination."

"Used to be birthdays—" Pete looked around, seeking confirmation "—didn't it?"

"Anniversaries," offered Kyle.

"Hey!"

Everyone turned at the surprise in Henderson McGill's voice.

"There, Jim," he exclaimed, pointing at the wall just to the right of the lock control.

"Graffiti. Like the others. So what's so fucking interesting?"

"What's interesting, Mr. Thomas, is that this is signed."

It looked as though it had been written with a narrow-tipped green felt pen in an elegant, sloping, italic hand.

"Jim H." was all it said. And then three initials beneath it. "J.K.Z."

"My God!" breathed Jed Herne. "Has to be."

Jim punched his right fist into his left palm. "Why would General John Kennedy Zelig have written on the wall? Written my initials? It doesn't make any sort of sense."

Mac pointed at the writing. "General Zelig wasn't the kind of man to do a damn thing without good reason. You don't get to be head of the United States Air Force's space-research section by being real stupid. Zelig wrote that, then by God he had good reason for it."

"His writing?" asked Carrie.

Jim nodded. "Sure is. Green pen and those funny angular letters. No, it's Zelig. Why?"

"Code."

"How's that, Kyle?"

"I don't know, but it has to be. The security door opens on a four-digit code. Your first name and second name initial, Captain."

"Could be." Jim looked at the others. "Anyone got a better idea? No? Nor me. Let's give it a go."

He leaned forward and peered at the small display panel, then punched in a *J*, an *I*, an *M* and finally an *H*.

The dark screen above the coding buttons suddenly showed a message in yellow lettering: "Incorrect entry. Try again. Caution. Four incorrect entries will lead to security alert and will incapacitate locking mechanism."

"Shit!" Jeff Thomas glowered at Kyle Lynch. "Great idea, shit-for-brains!"

At that moment they all heard the sound of footsteps behind them, way toward the main entrance to the complex.

"Company," said Mac quietly.

"Could be help?" Pete looked at the other seven. "Well, it *could* be."

"Sure. Sure, and pigs might fly," said Carrie. "Don't see much airborne bacon passing by on the wing these days."

Now there were voices, talking and calling out urgently. Jim looked again at the controls, feeling everything slipping away from him.

On an impulse he pressed the same letters as before. This time in reverse.

The same thing happened, but with the additional warning that they had only two more attempts to get the security code right.

"We're like hogs on ice here," said Mac, fists clenched. "Don't even have a pocket knife between us. If it's the ones took out the guards, we're all dead meat."

"Numbers," said Kyle suddenly. "The letters are too obvious. Too obvious for a devious bastard like Zelig."

"Numbers?" said Jim. "Number for each letter, starting from the top of the alphabet. So *J* is ten. That one or zero? Then nine, then thirteen and then eight. Ten, nine, thirteen and eight. That's six different digits."

"Try them, for fuck's sake!" hissed Jeff Thomas. "They're getting nearer."

The voices had stopped, but the boots were closing in.

Jim pressed one and zero and nine and one again, watching the screen above the keys.

"Incorrect! Warning, you have only one more attempt to enter the code correctly."

"This way!" The voice was distinct, putting the speaker only a couple of doors away from them, along the corridor.

· It didn't sound like a friendly voice, and Jim Hilton wasn't about to take a chance on it.

"No," he said quietly. "The last digits. Must be. Zelig wouldn't have given all four letters otherwise. Must be the last digits of the four number equivalents. Here we go."

It was a dead-end corridor.

No place to hide.

No place to run.

"Do it," urged Mac.

"Zero, nine, three, eight."

For a dozen heartbeats, nothing happened. The screen went blank, then two words appeared on it: "Code accepted."

Then there was a hissing of powerful hydraulic gears, behind the reinforced walls of concrete and steel, and the heavy door slid sideways.

"Quick," said Jim.

They rushed and jostled inside the familiar lobby to their quarters. Mac was last, though, turning and stabbing a finger onto the red emergency button that closed the door again. After a moment's hesitation, it began to move shut, agonizingly slowly.

Jim stood near the shrinking gap, peering into the passage outside. He saw a flicker of movement and heard shouting.

"Come on," he urged in a whisper, but the door still stood seven or eight feet open.

A rough, strident voice called out. "Hold it!"

A man appeared around the bend of the corridor, with a sawed-down scattergun cradled in his arms. He wore casual clothes, looking like a weekend hunter. Jim had time to notice a plaid shirt with a thermal vest underneath it and that the stranger was heavily bearded and long-haired.

"Hold the bastard door!"

The gun was leveled, barely fifty feet away.

Jim Hilton was frozen, aware that the gap was still five feet, and that an ominous grinding sound came from the door's gearing.

It was moving more slowly.

There were half a dozen men now in the passage, all holding firearms, yelling menacingly.

Then the door stopped, jammed open.

13

The gap was about the width of a man's shoulders, but to Jim's horrified eyes it looked as though a truck could be driven through it.

There was the boom of a gun, and he ducked away as lead starred out, mostly hitting the steel door with a crunching blow.

"Get the bastards!" The voice from the corridor had a chilling, murderous quality.

Mac, at Jim's elbow, jabbed again and again at the button to close the door. "Close, you son of a bitch!" he screamed.

There was the crackle of small arms, underlaid with the deeper sound of shotguns. Several rounds sliced through the gap, exploding against one of the walls of the lobby, over the heads of the *Aquila*'s crew.

A number of high-velocity bullets struck the door, ringing like a gong. Their collective impact made the whole structure shudder, jarring the jammed gears and freeing the powerful hydraulic mechanism so that it began to close again.

"Keep down!" yelled Jim Hilton, seeing that Pete and Jed were about to get up.

The indecision had gone, and he could feel the adrenaline surging through his body. His hand ached with the desire to hold a pistol and return fire at the butchers gathered outside the door.

The gap shrank to a few inches, and then vanished to nothing.

"There's a locking control," said Carrie, sounding amazingly calm. "Red lever on the right."

Mac threw it down, and the sign above flashed "Manual control operated."

It was suddenly silent. Two more shots rang off the other side of the door, but the noise was strangely muffled, like the tolling of a bell far under the sea.

"Is there another entrance?" Jeff Thomas was on his feet, grinning like a maniac, fresh blood seeping from the deep gash across his cheek. "Come on...you guys know this fucking warren better than I do. Is there another way in or out?"

Jim answered him. "Emergency exit. We're fifty feet under the base here. There's an air lock and ladder to a heavy steel cover. Hand-operated ring lock on it. Be almost impossible to break in that way unless you nuked it."

"So we're safe. For a while."

Jim nodded. "Yeah, for a while. Might as well make the most of what we got while we're in here. Looks like none of the raiders made it inside. The generator's still doing its stuff. We got light and heat, fresh air and water. Should be plenty of processed food. Baths. Beds."

Jeff Thomas gave Steve Romero a high five. "All right!"

"Guns?" asked Pete Turner. "Don't remember seeing any around."

Jim nodded slowly. "Had my own automatic in my locker. If it's still safe there. But it won't carry us very far against a dozen men with rifles and 10-gauge shotguns."

"Least they can't break in here after us." Mac said.

Jim nodded. "Just for a few hours, I'd settle for being where we are. Think about crossing any bridges later."

AFTER THEY'D TAKEN BATHS, they dug into the living quarters. Each of them went to their own personal lockers, coming across clothes and other items that they hadn't seen for over two years.

Jim looked around at the shocked and strained expressions on everyone's faces. "Listen up. We all got small cabins. Take what you got and get some privacy. Then we can meet up again in the dining section in an hour."

Each of them found the process of going through their possessions almost overwhelmingly painful. Normally, after a mission, it would have been sheer delight, a pleasure to come across the souvenirs of family and friends, knowing that they would soon be seen again.

But after the spilled-blood look of the planet when they'd broken through into the atmosphere and the discovery of the inexplicable destruction and deaths around Stevenson base, the anticipatory pleasure had been replaced by fear.

A gut-churning, cold fear.

Jim found the drawings of himself and the *Aquila* that Heather and Andrea had drawn for him. Heather's was neat and linear, in black and white. Andrea's was in bright colours, shaded and blurred. Both had written their messages of love to him. They'd been nine then. Now they were both eleven.

If they were alive.

Steve had a postcard from Leadville in Colorado, showing a crazy old crone peeking from a log cabin. Baby Doe Tabor. With its sad little tale of family tragedy and death. It was from his son, Sly, posted a week before the *Aquila* had taken off for deep space. The boy had been just sixteen, still living in Aspen with his thrice-married mother.

"Hot and high here, Dad. Hiked some good trails on my own. Mom seems—" something was thickly crossed out "—and sends all her love, Let the eagle fly high, Dad, and come back safe to your son. Lotsalove from Sly."

Steve sat on his narrow bed in his cramped quarters and cried.

Jeff Thomas flicked through a small folder of family pictures. His father, frail and pale, standing and blinking at the camera, outside the Madonna Inn, in San Luis

Obispo. Various girls, some bumping and grinding for the snapshots.

There was a tiny round mirror, with raised edges, and an engraving of a dew-tipped rose below its surface. Jeff could see the faint residual traces of white powder crusted around the lip of the mirror and he wished, profoundly wished, that he had a little brown glass vial of coke to carry him along the next few hours. But drugs on the space-research base was almost the ultimate crime.

The mirror showed him the jagged scar across his face and the massive purple bruising around his broken nose, already yellowing at its borders.

"Bastard," he said.

Henderson McGill was standing in his bedroom, holding a set of blue dumbbells, doing wrist pulls with them, horrified at his own weakness.

He dropped to the floor and tried some one-arm push-ups.

Kyle had a lethal hunting knife in his hand. He was stroking the razored steel edge against his cheek, his eyes far away.

Carrie was lying back on her bed, irritated that the hair dryer wasn't working properly. The main thing that she'd taken from her personal locker was a Walkman, with earphones and lithium batteries. Now it was playing through the long, slow darkness of Pachelbel's Canon in D.

Like Steve, she was crying.

Pete was working out in his room. His martial-arts training had never been put to practical use, but he was always ready. Now, with gunmen outside the heavy door, this might be the chance he'd been waiting for. Since Janey's death he'd practiced and practiced, hoping he would one day face overwhelming odds. Kill some of the vermin, and then be killed himself. So he could go join his dead wife.

Now it might soon be happening, and Pete Turner would be ready. As he turned and kicked and punched the air, he was smiling.

Jed Herne was patiently rubbing surgical liniment into his damaged knee.

Jim Hilton had found something else in his locker, and he had laid it on his side table.

Thirty-five ounces of blued steel. Six-inch barrel. Single-action revolver, the chamber holding six rounds of .44 full-metal-jacket ammunition. The hammer was low set, deeply checkered and wide spurred. Wide trigger. Full-length ejector shroud and a cushioned grip with engraved walnut inserts.

The Ruger Blackhawk Hunter, Model GPF-555.

It had cost Jim nine hundred and fifty dollars, and he'd bought it three months before taking off from Stevenson.

There was a small box of ammunition. Forty-two rounds, he counted.

Everyone had changed, after the hot baths, into their own clothes, opting for casual comfort rather than style. Jeans were universal, with shirts or sweatshirts. Jim had dug out his hiking boots, though most of the others picked trainers. He also had on a thick jacket in patched browns, greens and grays that he used on his survivalist hiking trips. The pockets easily swallowed all the ammo for the powerful revolver.

He picked up the Ruger, feeling its familiar shape and balance, and leveled it at himself in the mirror on the far wall.

"Bang," he said.

AS THE HOUR CAME to its ending, Carrie and the seven men drifted toward the main dining section of mission control.

Jim perched on the edge of the table, the Ruger holstered on his right hip. A sheath knife balanced it on the left side of the belt.

"Right," he said.

"I have to get to see a doctor about my nose and this cut," said Jeff. "How's about some kind of transport off base?"

"Have to get past the guys with the rifles and shotguns," Mac said.

"You got your gun, Captain," said Jed Herne, wincing slightly as he lowered himself into one of the deep chairs around the walls.

"Sure. Six-shot revolver. Better than nothing, I guess."

"We get out that back exit," said Pete Turner, "and if they're there, we go down fighting."

"Simple, Peter. But not that effective." Carrie looked at Jim. "The radio?"

"Not working," replied Steve Romero. "Like on the ship. We just pick up plenty of nothing clear across all the wave bands."

"I want to try for home." Mac's voice broke into the silence, expressing what all of them were privately thinking.

There was a ragged chorus of agreement, stopping as Jim Hilton held up both hands.

"Yeah. Me, too. Need some thought and planning. There's plenty of hi-con food in the stores, travel packs, maps. No weapons. I just wish we had a better idea what's been happening here—or any damn idea at all."

Kyle half lifted a hand. "One thing's been bothering me. And I just realized what it is."

"What?"

The tall black navigator had been leaning against an empty coffeemaker. "Zelig's message. Left for us. For you, Skipper."

"Look, it's maybe better now to just call me 'Jim,' rather than 'Captain' or 'Skipper.' I'm not captain of anything now. But, yeah, you got a point there. Did Zelig leave it as they evacuated? Or..." He paused to think it through. "Did he come back here after... after whatever it was had happened? If he did, is there some other kind of message for us?"

There was.

14

Jim Hilton was furious with himself.

Though he wasn't the oldest of the crew—Mac had that dubious honor—he was certainly the most senior. Supposedly the most experienced and the best able to command.

But he hadn't figured it out as Kyle Lynch had. Zelig's message outside the door had been deliberately coded and made obscure, so the general by then must have been fully aware of the dangerous threat to the base.

And Jim knew in his heart that he'd slipped up badly in overlooking the possibility that there might be another message somewhere within the sealed section of the Air Force base. But then, he hadn't been used to thinking along conspiratorial lines.

His training had been running a starship and correlating the variety of experimentation on their missions.

"Could be a note or a tape," he said. "Might be in code."

"Zelig must have known that nobody had penetrated into our quarters," said Carrie. "So it might just be out in the open."

Steve Romero was the one to find it.

"Cassette player," he called. "Bit of paper stuck under the lid that says 'Play me.' That's all. Not signed, but it's Zelig's hand."

They gathered around.

Beyond the lobby there'd been some muffled banging on the doors, as though the attackers were trying to force entrance. But Jim was confident that they would never manage to break in.

As Steve reached to switch on the player, the overhead lights flickered, went out for a moment, then came on again.

Mac looked at Jim. "Could be the bastards are trying to get at the power supply. If they find the link between here and the nuke generator, we're in shit. Air and light and everything stops."

"Right. Turn on the tape. Better hear it before we lose it."

The red light came on, and the digital audiotape began to play. A faint hiss, then the familiar voice of General John Kennedy Zelig.

It was an unlikely voice, high and thin, like a querulous old man's, belying Zelig's robust manner and appearance.

"Greeting to Captain Hilton and the crew of the *Aquila*. Welcome back to Earth, or what's left of it. You've got this far, so you'll be cognizant that there've been some changes around the old place. This tape is the only way we could think to debrief you and give you some minimal information. But you must realize that you are in great danger in the base. I am recording this here, on the spot, in the middle of June. I have only a small armed guard with me and I shall stay the shortest time possible. So I won't waste words."

Steve pressed the Pause button. "The old bugger sounds frightened."

"Never." Pete Turner laughed. "Zelig wasn't frightened of anything."

Jim shook his head. "No, Steve's got something. There's real strain in the voice. Said we were in danger, so he must have been when he made this tape for us. Carry on, Steve."

The story that Zelig rattled off for them, in his dry, flat voice, kept them totally silent.

The population of Earth had been growing far too fast for far too long, and agrarian scientists had been concentrating their efforts on improving production of basic foodstuffs. Cereals were being developed to produce their own proteins. Pulses were grown in laboratory complexes that had extra nodules on their root clusters, effectively giving them their own tiny nitrate factories.

Hand in hand with peaceful developments walked the military scientist, looking for newer ways of waging and winning wars.

"A plant bacteriologist in Leeds, in England, discovered a mutant gene that produced toxins in plants similar to cancer in humans. The spores were wind- and water-borne, almost invisible and undetectable. Unstoppable."

The lights went off again, and the tape stopped. This time it was several seconds longer before power was restored.

Jim made a decision. "Hold it, Steve. Listen, people. If they cut us off, then we have to get out fast. Out the rear exit . . . and they might be waiting for us. And we're not ready. Take ten. Get clothes and packs. Sleeping bags. One-man tents each. Water and as much hi-concentrate food as you can reasonably carry. Anything else that might be useful such as matches, compasses, maps if you can find any. Use your common sense. Meet here in ten minutes, ready to back-country it.''

JIM SENT KYLE to the stores again to find a waterproof tarpaulin. Jed had overloaded himself and had to drop some of the food packs. Jeff Thomas had gone to the opposite extreme and was carrying as little as possible.

When they had all gathered around the cassette player again, Jim nodded. ''Right. Switch on the tape again, Steve. And everyone keep ready for a fast move.''

Zelig sounded more tense. ''Seems we might be getting company in a few minutes. So hear this. The plant cancer works so fast that a green and healthy crop can be dead and rotting the next morning. It produces a strange color alteration as it kills. Green turns red, like spilled blood.''

''Earthblood,'' whispered Carrie.

"Before you took off on the latest mission, you might have heard something about trouble between Kurdistan and the alleged border violations with southern Iraq. That is, if you weren't too busy reading the comic strips."

"Was that a joke from Zelig?" breathed Kyle Lynch, disbelievingly.

"The situation deteriorated with accusations of chemical and nerve warfare."

Jim suddenly recalled the last recorded news transmissions that they'd heard on board the *Aquila*. They'd mentioned this conflict.

Zelig was continuing. "Someone, I believe we will never know who, stole the research data from England along with samples of the genetic cancer. There was a border skirmish some days later and during it, so our Intelligence reports, someone released this virulent toxin."

"Oh, Jesus," said Pete Turner quietly.

"The question of responsibility is now purely academic."

After a momentary darkening of the lights and a wavering of the tape, Zelig's voice resumed again.

"Bandits coming closer. Start winding this up. Anyway, ladies and gentlemen, the poison spread like a wildfire. The Irish potato famine was an agricultural blink in the cosmic eye compared to what came to be called Agent Earthblood. Death came swiftly, from the humblest sphagnum and lichen to the tallest redwoods."

"Those red forests," Mac said.

"Overnight the world's food supply was finished. Within a month the whole planet was infected."

There was a booming sound from the main entrance, making everyone start and look around. But it wasn't repeated.

"Seaweed died. Food chains were severed, and the ecosystem collapsed. Animals starved. Then people began to starve. New York, as an example, had less than a week's reserves of food. The cities emptied into the country..." There was a pause and some noise in the background, then Zelig went on. "I have to go in a moment. There were deaths, deaths on a colossal scale. When you get away from Stevenson, you'll find a grievously changed world. Not just thousands of dead but millions upon millions. By the time you hear this, it may be that the population of the entire United States can be measured in only tens of thousands, scattered far and wide. Keep away from cities, Captain Hilton. Society is gone, industry terminally finished." They heard Zelig calling to someone else. "Right, Major. Get the men on double alert ready to move."

Jim looked at the others in the low-ceiling room with him, seeing his own sick horror reflected in everyone's faces.

"Not a dream," said Mac, eyes like iced marble. "Fucking nightmare."

"That's how it is," continued General Zelig. "Finish. End. But if you are hearing this, then you have survived. Three months before you listen to this message, at the time of your scheduled return, you know that I, your commanding officer, am alive and reasonably well. And there are others. Contingency plans have always been laid to cover any sort of disaster eventuality. Even one as unlikely as Earthblood. There are..."

Half the lights in the underground bunker went off, and the humming of the air-conditioning ceased. The tape faltered, then resumed.

"...a number of men and women..." Half the remaining lights clicked off, casting the whole complex into an undersea gloom.

"Must be the guys with the guns." Steve looked at Jim. "Get out?"

Jeff Thomas was already picking up his backpack, struggling to get the straps adjusted across his shoulders. "Come on."

Jim shook his head. "Wait. Zelig's getting to the wire. Sounds like there might be some kind of a plan or something."

The tape had halted, but now it began again hesitantly. But there seemed to have been an important gap in it.

"The place for this hasn't yet been finalized. But contact can be made in a variety of ways. First priority is to reach Calico by the middle of November, when..."

The explosion that blew in the outer security doors was devastating, sending a blast of heat and choking dust swirling through the astronauts' quarters. The lights instantly blinked off.

15

Jim was knocked sideways, falling into the cassette player. He was vaguely aware of a metallic crashing noise, but he was too busy getting onto hands and knees to pay any attention to it. Behind him there was shouting, and he glimpsed torches slicing through the wreathing dust.

Someone trod on his fingers, making him yelp in pain.

"They're in, Jim!" shouted Mac from somewhere toward the sleeping quarters.

"Get everyone out—" he caught himself, not wanting to give too much away "—out the way we agreed, Mac. Packs and all."

"How about you?"

"Be right with you."

The Ruger Blackhawk Hunter was in Jim Hilton's hand, his index finger snug on the broad trigger of the single-action revolver.

It had never felt so right.

There was scuffling movement all around him. Once he'd recovered his bearings, Jim knew his own heavy pack was lying close by the double doors that opened through toward the air lock and the rear exit.

Now he waited, crouched by the overturned music system, left hand loosely holding his right wrist in the approved shooter's stance.

"This way, Harry!"

The boom of a shotgun sounded near the lobby, followed by a yell of rage or pain. Jim guessed one of their attackers had been trigger-happy.

His father had fought in Nam, wriggling in the stinking blackness of the tunnels around Cu Chi. The experience had messed up his mind, and he had woken with nightmares of the hand-to-hand butchery, right up until Jim was ten years old. Then his father had gone out into the garage at three o'clock in the morning, when the blood runs slow and the soul suffers through its dark night.

He'd hung himself.

But he'd talked about killing to his son. Talked in the long drunken evenings, as the level dropped lower in the bottle of Southern Comfort and the pain glared through his eyes.

"It's a skill like any other, son. But I pray to Jesus Christ Almighty that you never, never, never have to learn it."

The men with the flashlights were hesitating, just on the other side of the doorway into the dining quarters. They were crowded together in the cramped passage less than twenty feet from where Jim Hilton was waiting silently for them . . . waiting to begin learning his father's skill.

"Get in!"

"Why don't you get in yourself!"

"Get the hell in, or I'll put you down on your fucking back!"

"Yeah?"

"Yeah. Get inside. We got the torches. Looks like they don't."

Jim waited. Behind him he could hear the others, doing their best to keep quiet as they headed for the exit.

"What if they got guns?"

"They'd have used them when we nearly had 'em trapped, wouldn't they?"

"Yeah," came the answer grudgingly.

"So, get in. We're all right behind you."

Jim fought to slow his breathing, steadying the barrel of the revolver on the juddering beams of the flashlight.

"Wait," he whispered to himself. "Not too soon. Wait."

The first man was inside the doorway, shining his flashlight around, but the pall of smoke and dust bounced it back at him.

Now they were crowding the door, made more confident by the silence and the lack of response from their trapped victims.

Jim Hilton tightened his index finger on the Ruger's trigger. The jolt ran through his wrist, past his elbow, to the shoulder. In the confined space the crack of the explosion was surprisingly loud.

He didn't hesitate but fired again and again, pumping four bullets into the jostling men. Aiming, as he'd been told by his father, a little above the belt buckles.

"That way you should manage to hit something kind of important. Only person tries to aim for the head is the real amateur... or the real professional."

Above the thunder of the big handgun, there was screaming, yells of pain and shock.

And, Jim noticed in passing, fear.

It made him feel good.

Someone shouted, above the panic. "Get the hell out of here!"

There was a trampling of feet and the lights disappeared, leaving the room in total darkness.

Jim stood up, the warm gun steady in his right hand. There was someone moaning close by the door. A bubbling, pitiful sound, like a kid blowing down a straw into a strawberry milk shake.

Words were frothing through the cries, but he couldn't understand any of them.

He was tempted to reload the Ruger, but he had the uneasy feeling he might drop the ammunition. It still held two full-metal-jacket rounds, one nestling snugly under the hammer.

Keeping the gun in his left hand, Jim stopped and fumbled for the straps of the heavy pack. He picked it up and moved cautiously across the room, heading for the passage leading toward the air lock and the hidden exit, and his seven companions.

There was a burst of gunfire from behind him, but he didn't hear any shots come even close to him. He guessed they were wild shots triggered by panic.

The longer the hunters stayed outside and blasted pointlessly into the darkness, the better the chances of escape.

Now, ahead of him, Jim could hear the others, voices snarling in suppressed anger. One was Mac, and the other sounded like Jeff Thomas.

Taking a chance that the pursuers weren't close, Jim called out. "What's going on?"

Carrie answered first. "Jeff's on the ladder and he can't open the locking wheel and he won't move to let Mac try it."

"I can do it!"

"He can't."

Jim felt someone directly ahead of him. "Who's this? Pete?"

"No, Kyle."

"Let me through."

The tension of having just killed was getting to him, and he had an insane urge to start giggling. But he swallowed it down and pushed past into what he could feel was a confined space.

"It's me, Mac," said the bulky figure directly in front of him.

"You get anyone?" asked Jed Herne from the left side of the air lock.

Jim didn't answer. He still held the revolver in his hand, the pack slung on one shoulder. "Get off and let Mac do it, Jeff," he said, trying to keep his voice calm.

"I'll do it soon."

"Get down now."

"Don't tell me what to do. We're back on land, your mandate expired."

"Now, Jeff, or I'll put a .44 up your ass."

There was a moment of infinite stillness.

"A dozen men are out there gunning for us. I killed four of them, and that leaves two bullets in the chamber. I won't tell you again. Down now, or you're dead."

The journalist couldn't conceal his dismay. "You'd really do it, wouldn't you, Hilton?"

The click of the hammer coming back was surprisingly loud in the stillness.

"All right, I'm coming. But it's jammed tighter than a nun's—"

"Now," said Jim.

There was a scuffling noise as Jeff slid down the iron ladder. Mac handed his pack to Pete Turner and climbed up, feeling in the pitch dark for the locking ring.

"Don't forget your gear," said Jim, quietly letting the hammer down on the revolver.

"Yeah, sure."

"Had no choice, Jeff." Jim added, wishing that he didn't feel the moral weakness of his position quite so strongly.

"Look good when the story breaks in the *West American,* won't it, *Captain?*"

"From what General Zelig said, there might not be too many editions of your paper around right now."

"Probably just blowing in the wind, Jeff," said Carrie Princip.

"How is it, Mac?"

"Hasn't been opened in a year or more." He grunted with the effort. "But I'm trying..."

Smugly Jeff Thomas said, "Told you. It's jammed tight."

The voice from above was strained and tense. "Wrong, buddy. Moving." There was the dry squeaking of metal, then a faint hissing as the rubber seal around the round cover was broken. Fresh warm air came flooding in, with jagged blades of bright Nevada sunlight.

"Forgot it was morning," said Kyle. "Been in the dark so long."

Mac was standing on the top of the ladder, peering out under the rim of the manhole. "Nobody around," he said.

He threw it all the way open, and the tunnel filled with the dazzling sun.

"I'll get out. One of you pass up all the packs. Save blocking the ladder."

Jim backtracked a little along the tunnel, toward the main living quarters, but there was no sound of pursuit.

It took less than a minute for their packs to be handed out, followed by the other six men and Carrie. Jim Hilton took the captain's privilege of coming out last, still holding on to the Ruger.

"We can jam the lock," said Mac.

"How?"

"One of those boulders. Smash it in so they can't follow us out."

"Do it, Mac."

They were on top of a small bluff, with higher ground rising behind them. Beyond that was the main part of the Stevenson Air

Base, with its damaged runways and its burned-out buildings.

Ahead of them the land was gray desert, bare except for patches of sagebrush and mesquite. Away to the far east, about eighteen miles off, was Chimney Wells, the nearest community, small but with a highway that eventually led toward something that had once been civilization.

Jed Herne touched Jim on the sleeve as they watched Mac pounding the top of the metal lock with a granite rock.

"You really kill four of them, Skipper?"

"Yeah. Think so."

Then he knelt down in the dusty earth and threw up.

16

At Jim's suggestion they had crawled up to the top of the slope, careful not to show themselves against the skyline.

From there they could see all the way around, with no risk of anyone sneaking up on them. The Air Force base lay out to the west, like a damaged map, covered in burned smears.

"No sign of those bastards," said Kyle Lynch. "Think they're still trying to get out and follow us?"

"Maybe they've given up," replied Jim Hilton.

"Shame you didn't get any of their guns, Captain," said Pete Turner.

"Yeah...mind, I was sort of busy there." Mentally he cursed himself for not having the presence of mind in the darkness, the confusion and the urgent need to get away to think of it.

Carrie asked, "Now what?" and every face turned toward her. "Well, we heard the tape...most of it. Know that a disaster's wiped out most of the world while we were up there sleeping."

Steve Romero whistled through his teeth. "Just before they blew in the doors, it seemed like Zelig was giving us some sort of message."

Jed was massaging his knee, wiping beads of sweat from his forehead. "Said that we should get together some place."

"Middle of November," said Pete.

"Zelig named a place." Mac glanced round at the others. "Anyone remember it? The explosion's blown it out of my memory."

"Calico," said Jeff Thomas.

"Where's that?" asked Jim. "Isn't it a ghost town in Colorado?"

"California." He lay back and closed his eyes. "Wish I'd brought my shades. Yeah, it's just off I-15, few miles east of Barstow. Old mining township, done up in the late part of the twentieth century as a tourist attraction."

"You know it?" asked Jim.

"Sure. Did an interview there once with a senator."

"We got around nine weeks to the middle of November." Mac rubbed the inside of his arm where he'd been burned in the crash landing. "Fact is, I'd like to try and find what's happened to Jeanne, Angel and the kids." He stared at Jim Hilton. "You got any objections to that, Captain?"

"If he has, he'll shoot you, so watch your step, Mac," Jeff said with a grin.

"I told you. Calling me by my rank's pointless now, Mac. I can't order you to do anything. Not anymore."

"But you're the man with the gun," Jeff said pointedly.

"Sure. And I have a feeling that this brave new world we've dropped into might be ruled by the gun rather than the dollar."

Jed Herne grinned at him, making a suggestive motion with his right hand. "Sounds like you've been reading some old-fashioned science fiction, Skip . . . I mean, Jim."

"All right, but if we're going to split up, then I want you to go with the best advice I can give."

"What's this advice, Jim?" Pete Turner asked.

Far below them they all saw the line of men threading out from under the crest of the hill. Everyone edged back under cover, taking care not to draw the hunters' attention.

"They're giving up," said Kyle.

The group was moving steadily westward, toward the broken perimeter fence and eventually the distant state line with California.

A pair of coyotes broke from behind the burned-out wreckage of the *Aquila* and began to lope away northward. Several of the men raised rifles and opened fire. The puffs of white smoke were clearly visible, though the distance almost silenced the sound. It was possible to see the tiny spurts of sand around the fleeing animals, but none of the shots hit home and the coyotes escaped into the brush.

"Want to go back down and get your sunglasses, Jeff?" asked Pete Turner.

"If what that pinch-mouthed prick, Zelig, said is true, I'll be able to find myself a pair at the first store I see."

"You were going to give us some advice, Jim?" said Mac, sitting down cross-legged. "Then let's get on with it."

"Yeah. Listen up, everyone. This might well be the last time we get to be all together. Seems to me the only sensible course is to believe what we heard from the general. Everything's gone to hell while we were away."

"Maybe things got better since he left that cassette," said Jed Herne.

"Could be they haven't." Carrie looked at the others. "Guys with rifles and shotguns breaking into the heart of the base and trying to slaughter us all!" The note of anger and disbelief rode in her voice. "That's getting better, is it, Jed?"

Jim held up his hand to check the argument from developing.

"Most important thing is to get hold of guns. And don't hesitate to use them when you have to. Killing's a skill like any other. The way society's gone, you won't get too many second chances. Carry food and water when you can. Basic survivalist skills will help get us through."

"I want to get moving, Jim," said Mac. "Miles to go before I sleep."

"No deep woods out there," Kyle Lynch said quietly. "Just a lot of bloodred, dead trees."

"We've all got enough hi-concentrate food for a couple of weeks, more if you're real careful. And we all got water for a day but not much longer, even if you are careful."

Jeff was staring at Jim Hilton as he spoke. "Why don't you let someone else have your gun?"

"What?"

"You have all the best fucking skills. Outdoorsman and backwoodsman and survivalistman. You can make it better than any of us. I'm a city boy. I could really use that big mother on your hip."

Jim smiled. "Then come and take it off me, Jeff. If you want it bad enough."

"No way." Jeff shrugged, holding out his hands. "No way, Jim."

"Then you don't want the Ruger badly enough, Jeff. Remember that."

They agreed to try to meet again in the ghost town of Calico around November 15.

All that remained was to decide how they'd split up, following Jim's insistence that nobody should think of traveling alone.

It didn't take long to split into groups, and then they broke up the unit that had been the crew of the *Aquila,* uncertain whether they would ever get together again.

17

There was a battery-operated clock on the wall of the cabin, showing the date, as well as the time.

It was a little after five in the evening of October 3, 2040.

Jed had found an antique Winchester rifle in the main bedroom, bringing it along the hallway to the small, neat kitchen. He tried to lever the action, but it was jammed solid and he threw the useless weapon down in the corner.

"Damnation! Means them ornery scalpin' Apaches might come a'sneakin' up on us and we're fresh out of firepower."

Jeff Thomas was opening a can of tomatoes and he glanced over his shoulder at his colleague. "How come I got the short straw and you?" he said disgustedly. "All you can think of are those old Western vids. Now, if Carrie had been my traveling partner..." He allowed the sentence to drift away into the late-afternoon quiet.

"Yeah, the feeling's mutual, buddy."

It was a week since they'd parted from their friends on the high bluff overlooking the Stevenson Air Force Base, splitting into pairs, heading off in different directions.

Jed Herne had his roots clear across the continent, in South Strafford, Vermont. But he'd left his home state when he went to college ten years earlier and only returned once. Relations had been difficult between himself and his widowed mother, and time and distance hadn't improved things.

The end had come eight years ago, when he'd struggled through appalling weather to make Thanksgiving with his mother. It had taken him two days in a rented four-by-four when blizzards closed down the airports. He'd also had a virulent attack of tonsillitis and a raging fever.

When he reached the trim white-board house, up a side street from the general store, his mother had reluctantly opened the screen door and peered querulously out at him.

"Least you could've got your hair cut," she'd said.

Jed had spun on his heel and gotten straight back into the rented vehicle and driven away to rejoin his colleagues on the New York Giants.

He'd never spoken to his mother again after that day and hadn't gone home for the funeral when cancer took her three years later.

Since he didn't have any real reason to go anyplace, Jed had been more or less happy to keep Jeff Thomas company.

The journalist was eager to get to his apartment in San Francisco, close by Fisherman's Wharf, and had also talked about going via San Luis Obispo, where he'd left his ailing father.

"Want some of these?" He offered the opened can to Jed, with a green-handled spoon sticking out of the top.

"Yeah, I guess. Anything else left in the cupboards? Looks like they cleared it out when they left."

"They probably killed their dog before they went. There's about a dozen cans of Bark 'n' Bite."

Jed munched on the warm tomatoes. "Don't think I'm ready for dog food yet."

"There's some pasta. Could light a fire and heat some water."

Jed decided that he'd reached about the halfway mark and handed the can back. "Here," he said. "Boned and deflavored by our chef, for your dining pleasure."

He went back into the living room, dimly lit behind the drawn drapes. Jed was still limping slightly, favoring his weakened knee, and he sat down on a long sofa upholstered in a maroon Naugahyde.

It had been cold in the past couple of days, and there was a dusting of snow on the high, jagged peaks of the Sierra Nevada towering above them to the west.

He heard the empty can clattering in the dusty sink. Then the journalist called from the kitchen, "Going to have a look around before dark."

"Sure."

The back door slammed, setting some brightly painted wind chimes tinkling above the television in the corner.

Jed stretched out, resting his muddied boots on a low table, moving a neat pile of

Sierra Club magazines. Walking didn't come too easily after his ligament operations, and the past week had seen them do a daily hike of twenty to thirty miles. Now he felt bone weary, ready to crash out into one of the pair of single beds in the chintzy room just along the corridor.

He let his mind drift back over the past seven days, since the group of eight astronauts had separated and gone in four different directions.

Within the first tiring hour, he and Jeff had realized that Zelig's message was true. Virtually all the sagebrush and mesquite around the runway was dead, dry and brittle, their stems and leaves carrying the faint hint of the toxic red plant cancer.

As soon as they reached the nearest highway, intending to head north and then cut across the Sierras around Lake Tahoe, they'd encountered the first human signs of the mega disaster.

A stalled car, all four doors open, with two corpses inside it.

Someone had stolen the shoes off the male body, and the inside of the vehicle had been searched, opened luggage tipped everywhere. Both the woman and the man had been shot at close range. The former with a single round through the back of the neck and her companion through the mouth. The rear of his skull had been blown apart, blood and brains crusted and black across the roof of the car.

"Ran out of gas. No food. He shot her and then himself," suggested Jeff Thomas. Jed had been badly shaken by the discovery and didn't argue with the interpretation of the scene.

The gun had been missing.

They hadn't seen a living human being until well into the fourth day, heading along the pavement of Highway 95 toward Hawthorne. It had rained during the previous late afternoon, and they'd taken the opportunity to top up their water bottles at a frothing stream.

There'd been forty or fifty stalled vehicles along the way, many of them burned out, most with bodies close by. The corpses had all been weeks or months old, the skin dried and the lips peeled away. Many showed the unmistakable marks of having met violent deaths.

Jeff had been unusually subdued. "If it's like this out in the boonies, think what it's going to be like in the towns and the cities."

Then they'd encountered the first of the barricades, on the outskirts of Hawthorne. A barrier of trucks was blocking the highway, with a handful of armed men standing near them, watching their approach.

"Close enough," one of them had shouted.

"Can we pass through?" Jed was regretting that they hadn't had a chance to obtain weapons. These men with the guns called the shots, but even one armed man would be superior to them.

"Where you come from?"

"South."

"Vegas?"

"No. Why?"

"Plague there. Seen some of them, black swellings in their arms and groins."

"Can we pass through?" Jeff Thomas had yelled.

"No."

"Why not?"

"Just 'cause we say not. Strangers don't get in here. No food."

Jeff had been starting to talk again when Jed nudged him. "Don't tell them we got food. They could kill us for that."

Jeff had nodded at his whisper, looking toward the barrier, sixty yards ahead of them.

"Can we go around?"

The barrel of the rifle had waved toward the west, toward the looming hills.

"That way, stranger, and don't try sneaking in at night. You'll get caught by one of our vigilante patrols and shot on sight."

"Friendly bastards," Jeff had said under his breath.

"Do like they say. Head up into the higher country." Jed had tugged at Jeff's sleeve. "Come on. Before they get interested in our backpacks."

The men with the guns had watched them as they picked their way up a narrow trail among stunted, dead birches until they were out of sight.

The only consolation as they had walked through the endlessly dreary landscape of blackened and dying trees was the streams of fresh, clean water that tumbled from the peaks.

When they were clear of the northern edge of the township, Jeff had pointed to something below them. "What's that?"

It looked like a huge pile of tangled wood. Thick trunks around six feet long, with smaller, thinner branches stuck out at odd angles. One whole side of the jumble of dark wood was blackened as though someone had tried to burn it out.

"Cords of kindling," Jed had suggested. "Going to need plenty of wood around these parts once winter comes and there's no electricity."

Jeff had a small pair of powerful binoculars in his pack and he'd rummaged for them. Shuffling his feet on the narrow trail, he'd slowly turned the focus wheel, whistling between his teeth as he'd tried to focus on the woodpile.

"Oh, shit," he'd said very softly.

Jed had guessed then what they were looking at before he took the glasses and checked for himself.

"Figure that must be the rest of the good folks of Hawthorne," he'd said, viewing the pile of ragged, scorched corpses. Dozens upon dozens, jumbled with a dreadful lack of dignity, men and women and children, all unburied together.

"Weren't enough left alive to dig graves for them," Jeff had said. "You can still see the tracks of a big dozer where they collected them up and then just shoved them together."

Jed had researched the Final Solution to the "Jewish problem" in the Second World War for his master's degree. The boneyard below had brought back pictures of sweating, booted SS guards dragging fragile skeletons to death pits in Auschwitz and Belsen.

Now, here, in the United States of America.

JEFF THOMAS CAME BACK into the kitchen of the isolated cabin. Jed noticed that the journalist was looking remarkably better for a week's trekking. His podgy one-sixty-five had fined down to about closer to one-fifty, and his usual pallor had been replaced by a healthier color under the fall sun.

His temperament also seemed to have changed. On the *Aquila* he'd been way short of being Mr. Popular, with his constant bitching and moaning and his insistence that his paper's massive financial contribution to the project gave him special privileges. In the past three or four days, despite obvious discomfort from the broken nose, Jefferson Lee Thomas had been much better company.

"Nothing around."

"Wonder how the Earthblood virus affected animals and snakes and all? Would be good for the scavengers for sure."

"Saw that big rattler yesterday, when we hit off up this side trail. More scared of us than we were of it."

The cabin was almost invisible, even from the dirt road that they'd been using, traveling roughly parallel to the highway. Both men had realized that their best hope of finding shelter and maybe even food was to search out this sort of dwelling, untouched by the refugees from the towns desperate for food.

It was also a place where they weren't likely to encounter any bands of marauding hunters.

As night fell, they bolted the doors and locked the wrought-iron shutters tight. Jed lay in the narrow, damp bed, watching the pattern of moonlight moving across the ceiling.

"Jeff?"

"Yeah?"

"Your father, are we going to try and find him? After visiting your place in San Francisco?"

A long stillness was the only answer for a while.

"Devil of a way to walk it, Jedediah, my sporting friend."

"Maybe we'll find some sort of transport by then and some gas."

The figure in the other bed rolled on its side, wheezing a little through the displaced septum. "He was dying when we took off. They were talking a couple of months. Odds are real long against him still being in the land of the living."

"Don't you want to find out?"

"Not that much. My old man was a miserable bastard. If I could pick up a phone and call the hospital in San Luis Obispo, then I'd do it. Walk three hundred miles for one of his smiles... Thanks, Jed, but no thanks."

The room became filled with Jeff's steady snoring.

Jed wished he'd been able to use his electrical skill to get the power on in the cabin, though there was the danger that lights glowing up the hillside might attract unwanted company.

But even he couldn't conjure gasoline from thin air. It looked as if the previous occupants of the place had made their plans carefully, taking their personal possessions and draining every last spoonful of gas from the generator at the rear of the two-car garage.

At their present rate of progress, it would take Jed and Jeff weeks to get up to San Francisco. And that wouldn't leave them enough time to return south and hike to meet up with the others in Calico in the middle of next month.

Jed slipped toward sleep, his mind occupied in wondering where the other six were at that precise moment and what they were all doing.

18

The needle on the fuel gauge was quivering close to E.

The big Volvo truck was thundering eastward along state Highway 146, toward Placerville in western Colorado. Steve Romero and Kyle Lynch had soon made their own discovery that small roads were a better and safer bet than risking interstates where the natives—those that survived—were a lot less than friendly.

They'd disconnected the trailer and were pushing the pedal through the metal in the six-wheel cab, making the best speed they could on the straight stretches, slowing down on the sharp bends close to walking pace in case of road blocks.

It had been hard going as far as central Utah, not far from what used to be Capitol Reef National Park. Their lucky break had been finding a beat-up panel van pulled down off the highway, out of sight near a river. If Kyle hadn't been taken short and used the opportunity to fill his water bottle from the fast-flowing stream, they wouldn't have found it.

Every single mile of blacktop had its quota of abandoned vehicles. After checking the first twenty or so and finding every one had bone-dry tanks, they'd given up looking and walked on past the corpses of trucks and automobiles, with a scattering of dead humans lying everywhere.

After the first bodies, neither Kyle nor Steve paid much attention to the leathery, desiccated bodies. They were just another feature of the bloodred, dusty, alien landscape.

But the panel van was a find.

Someone had spent a lot of time and skill in decorating the sides and rear, customizing the interior with orange fur and a lot of leather and chrome. The panels were painted with ornate fire-breathing Oriental dragons in glittery shades of peach and rose and purple and gold.

And it had had half a tank of gas.

There had been no sign of its owner or driver, and the ignition key was still in place.

Steve hadn't hesitated, though Kyle had been worried about someone appearing from the dead bushes and opening up on them.

The van had carried them through until they came across the big truck.

Kyle had been behind the wheel, anxiously watching the gas situation when Steve had called to him to stop, then made him back up three hundred yards to a side trail between a couple of grain silos.

"Just caught the gleam of sunlight off the polished exhaust pipe," he'd said as they cruised around and found the Volvo.

They had also found what they assumed were the driver and his mate.

It had been a sad and ironic tableau, a scene that brought home to Kyle and Steve the appalling way that society had clawed its way to its ending.

The bodies had obviously been there for weeks, lying together by the cold ashes of a camp fire. The scavengers had been at them, stripping off the soft tissues, but enough was still left to tell the macabre tale.

Both men gripped knives in their gnawed fingers, a dark, rusted smear on each blade. Their arms were around each other's necks, one knee jammed between the taller skeleton's thighs.

On the ground at their side was the item that had obviously provoked the fatal fight. Part of the label had disintegrated, and the metal was discolored and dented.

Kyle had picked the small can up, peering at what remained of the label.

"It's ravioli," he'd said. "They killed each other over a tiny little stinking tin of horrible ravioli."

The truck had been a bulk-grain carrier, but it had been empty when they found it, and the silos were also echoingly empty.

Now it was beginning to look as though the two men were going to be left to their own devices again for progressing any farther toward their destination of Aspen.

The engine was starting to cough and splutter protestingly. They were on a long downgrade and Steve threw it out of gear to try to save the last spoonfuls of gas. The high vehicle cruised along, running between fields of dead corn, the stalks still carrying the bloodred tint that had become so familiar over the past seven days.

"Nearly done," he said.

"Back to walking. Boy, I sure love that walking." Kyle laughed. "Never thought that my life might depend on it."

It was late afternoon.

Around noon they'd passed through a nameless hamlet, a string of shacks hung out to dry along the highway, mostly with tarpaper roofs.

They'd been unoccupied, except for a skinny little black boy. He'd been standing by the side of the road, sucking his thumb, staring intently at the Volvo as it drew closer. A frayed T-shirt was all he wore, sticking out over his hunger-swollen belly and his pipe-thin legs. The boy's eyes were huge, seeming to fill the fragile death's-head face.

The eyes had turned to follow them all the way down the winding road.

"Maybe we could . . ." began Kyle Lynch, looking out of the open window.

"No," said Steve. "We've already seen enough dead and dying to know we can't stop. You don't know what's waiting behind the kid. Could be a handful of rednecks with 10-gauge shotguns.''

THE TRUCK ROLLED to a halt, its six wheels crackling over the dusty tarmac.

''We still have the best part of two hundred miles between us and Aspen,'' said Kyle, looking at the dog-eared Rand Mc-Nally they'd found in the jumbled sleeping quarters behind the driver's cab.

Steve pulled on the hand brake, opened his door and jumped down into the cool air. ''Two hundred. Manage twenty or thirty a day if the feet hold up. Still be two weeks to get there.''

''Right.'' Kyle climbed slowly down. ''You get so damn used to cruising the country in a powerful automobile, with the air-conditioning on high and the new ripped rock tape up full. Then one day you get up, and it's all gone. Jesus, man, you realize that it's all gone forever?''

''Sure. Here we are, on the third day of October in the year of Our Lord, 2040. Rain coming in from the west there. I want to...'' For a moment his voice broke, and he looked away.

''You all right, Steve?''

"Sure, thanks. Sure. Just got to wondering about Sly. Where's the kid now, right this moment? Think he's still alive, Kyle?"

"Look, you worry about things you don't know about, you'll go crazy, man."

"But he's only eighteen. And up there in Colorado, with . . . I don't know."

"Few days more, and we should be able to find out."

"Maybe we can pick up another truck or some kind of transport."

"We were lucky to find what we did. No point in looking anywhere near towns or main highways. Others'll have got there before us."

The metal of the Volvo's engine was cooling, the contracting metal making faint creaking, settling sounds. Far overhead they saw a lone hawk riding a thermal, wings spread, holding itself almost motionless against the cloudy sky.

"Hey! Maybe we should search the cab properly before we leave it. Could be they left some chocolate or some liquor there. I'll look."

Steve climbed back inside the truck, vanishing into the rear part behind the driver's seat. Kyle remained out on the side of the road, leaning against the front wheels, his pack by his feet.

He never saw the men approaching, just heard the sneering voice and the unmistakable click of a gun being cocked.

"Look what we got here. A nigger, all on his ownsome, with a big shiny truck."

19

The Kawasaki started to play up when they were close to Memphis, fifteen hundred miles and seven days into their transcontinental odyssey.

The 500 cc Norton was at least sixty years old, yet it continued to purr, day after day, never giving a moment's trouble, eating up the long miles eastward.

Pete Turner had picked the 350 cc twin Kawasaki and was already regretting it.

"Someone never looked after this baby properly," he moaned.

"Told you that old was best." Henderson McGill grinned.

The first of the eight to actually leave the base had been Jeff Thomas and Jed Herne, heading for San Francisco. Kyle Lynch and Steve Romero had gone next, Colorado bound. Jim Hilton and Carrie Princip had elected to travel together, on the shortest journey for any of them—to his home high up on Tahoe Drive in Hollywood.

Before Pete and Mac had left them, facing the longest trek, Jim had given them some considered advice, counsel that the first two pairs eventually learned from experience.

"Likely the best place to get any food or guns or transport is way off the beaten tracks. Cities are going to be boneyards. Towns will have been decimated. Smaller places won't welcome strangers. So look for isolated trails and hidden cabins. And don't put your trust in anyone."

Like many of the things Jim Hilton said, it had turned out to be good advice.

The first couple of days had been arduous. Pete's problems from the blow to the testicles made walking slow and difficult. Urinating was still painful, and he tried to drink as little water as possible. The result, predictably, was that he soon became dangerously dehydrated.

When they had stopped the second night to put up their little tents in a stand of dead aspens near a stream, Pete suddenly sat down, legs straight out in front of him.

"Ride her stone blind," he'd said in a flat voice. "Shit, I've got a hell of a headache, Janey."

Mac had knelt by him, patted him on the shoulder. "You been drinking enough, Pete?"

The eyes that had turned toward him lacked any spark, incurious as a dead moccasin snake.

"Drinking?"

"Here, have a few sips of this." Mac had held the bottle to his friend's lips, holding it firmly to steady it as some spilled over the front of the bleached denim shirt.

Ten minutes later the second pilot of the *Aquila* had recovered.

"Stupid," he'd said, wiping his dry mouth with his sleeve. "Once went hiking in the Grand Canyon and did the same damn thing. Too little to drink. Hot and dry and altitude and not even a baseball cap on. Thought I was going to die. Janey was real worried. She figured she'd have to go back up the trail and bring in the rangers with a chopper."

"What happened, Pete? How'd you get yourself out of it?"

"Decided I'd be embarrassed to be air-lifted. We were only about a third of the way down to the Colorado River. I tried doing fifty paces, then I sat and rested for a couple of minutes. Took a long while, but we made it."

"You still miss her, Pete, don't you? How long's it been?"

"Since Janey got murdered?"

"Yeah."

"You don't count it in days or weeks, months or years."

"What, then?"

Pete had shaken his head, eyes brimming with unshed tears. "Count it in evenings together lost. Afternoon hikes together, morning laughter together. And memories together, Mac. Lost, lost, lost. All of it lost."

THE TWO MOTORBIKES had been in a locked garage, behind the main street of a small, dusty town in eastern Nevada. It wasn't on the highway map, and there wasn't a single living soul there to tell them what it had once been called.

They found half a dozen dead, most of them looking as if they'd gone of natural causes. Like starvation.

Pete and Mac were already beginning to get used to the sight of death—and its smell.

A dry, unique odour. A mix of sweet and sour. Mac said it reminded him of brackish water standing in an abandoned root cellar.

The wind had been rising, early evening, as the two astronauts walked slowly along the main drag, past a couple of stores with broken windows. A screen door was blowing backward and forward at the Silver Garter Bar.

Pete trudged over and peered into the darkness. "Mess of broken bottles is all," he shouted back to Mac.

In a porch they came across a small pile of single-sheet newspapers, dateless, in large, smudged type, as if they'd been produced in a hurry, with a child's printing outfit.

Mac unfolded the top one, aware of the strange, brittle feel to it, suggesting it had been wet and dry a dozen times in the past few months.

Citizens! Panic is death. Martial law will be introduced in the next seven days unless the foolish exodus of refugees from all centers of population ceases. Government scientists are nearing success in countering the scourge of Earthblood, as the plant sickness is called. Once crops begin to grow again, all will be well. So, stay home and keep calm. Trust the government like you trust yourself. Relief food supplies will reach you any day now. Stay home and stay calm.

"Guess it was the end of the line by the time they tried this," Mac said. "Looks like they never even got to distribute these sheets."

"There's a stable down this alley." Pete led the way, while Mac dropped the paper he'd been reading. It drifted from side to side on the street, finally whirling away from the nameless township out into the pink-smeared desert wasteland beyond.

He followed on, easing the padded straps on the heavy backpack. The only consolation he could find was that it was getting slowly lighter as they worked through the hi-concentrate packaged foods from the space center.

The stable doors were wide open.

A horse's skull, picked bare, and four hooves were all that the stable held. A few flies, lazy and winter ready, were wandering through the gristle and gray bones on the head.

"Won't ride far on that." Mac laughed at his own joke, stopping as it echoed away up among the empty loft and forbidding rafters.

The unidentified hamlet was far enough from any major center of population to be safe from total looting. Even so, all the houses had been stripped of anything remotely edible and the stores were bare shelved.

But there was a dirt road along the back of the few houses.

That's where the garages were.

And that's where they found the Kawasaki and the Norton. Greased and polished and fueled up and ready to go.

THEY'D SEEN one odd thing.

On the powerful bikes they'd been able to make good time and distance, weaving between the stalled and crashed cars and trucks, avoiding the dry-stick, withered remnants of human beings along the highway.

Someone had shot at them from behind a camper van, near Little Rock, but they were going too fast and were too far away.

Farther on, near the hamlet of Beulah, Arkansas, about a hundred miles west of Memphis, there was a big poster offering recruitment to the United States Marine Corps.

But it had been defaced.

A quarter of the billboard had been covered in white paint. On it, in black, was the cryptic but neatly-painted message: "Tempest. Calico. 11-15. If this means you, then this means *you*."

Now the Kawasaki was giving trouble.

Pete had tried cleaning the plugs, but it hadn't done much good.

Also, both of the bikes were running low on fuel. The garage in the town with no name had jerricans of gas stacked on a bench, and they strapped two spare cans on each pillion before setting off again.

Now that was almost gone.

"Don't want to run out when we're halfway through what's left of Memphis, Tennessee," said Henderson McGill.

"Best we go around it."

"Yeah. North or south?"

"North'd be quicker," Pete said, studying the creased map.

"Looks easy?"

"Sure. Turn off north at Forrest City. Few miles to Wynne. Then east to bring us onto I-55. Seems easy on the map."

They rode on through endless fields on either side of them, fields that would have once been lush with a variety of crops. Yellow and gold and green.

Now they all looked the same, like something out of a documentary vid about the Dustbowl Depression of a hundred years earlier.

The land on both flanks of the blacktop was blasted, layered with tumbled, red, withered plants so rotted that it wasn't even possible to guess what they might originally have been.

They rode in single file, both keeping on the alert, ready for any kind of threat.

Back in Arkansas they'd found a smashed Harley, with the remains of its decapitated rider lying near the wreckage. Two telegraph poles on either side of the road held the rusting remnants of a thin wire that had obviously been strung across to catch the motorcyclist.

Pete was taking his turn in the lead and he suddenly held up his right hand, in their agreed warning sign. Mac throttled back, easing down to almost walking pace.

"What?" he shouted above the throbbing of the two engines.

"Look." Pete pointed to a hand-painted sign set up in a field about a quarter mile ahead of them: Cheap Gas In Hustonville. Two Miles.

The paint seemed fresh.

"Why not?" yelled Mac.

20

The warning lights were flashing on the corners of the bright yellow school bus.

Though Jim Hilton had tried every available switch and button, nothing seemed to turn them off. Since there wasn't a lot of traffic on the back road, it didn't much matter.

They hadn't actually seen any other traffic since they found the abandoned bus the previous afternoon.

Now they were closing in on Jim's Hollywood home, via winding back road from the north.

The first six days had been tough going. Carrie was having recurrent headaches, like vicious migraines. They'd needed to stop several times while she lay down, pale and sick, her face looking as if it had been rebuilt from slabs of candle wax.

The bright sunlight was particularly trying for her, and twice they'd had to rest up during the middle of the day then push on toward Los Angeles in the cool of the evening.

Water hadn't been easy to find at first. Then they'd learned to break into empty houses and top up their bottles from the standing tanks in the roof. The water was brackish, layered with dust and dead flies, but it kept them going.

The morning that they found the school bus they'd woken early, packed up their tents and had a light meal of hi-concentrate food.

Jim had thought it was safe to light a fire against the dawn's chill, using dry branches from a fallen sassafras. A thick column of pale smoke had risen into the still, cloudless sky.

It had brought them company.

Despite all of his survivalist training, Jim still got taken by surprise. He hadn't thought it necessary to post any sort of watch.

The cold voice from the shadows warned him not to turn around.

"Both of you keep real still. Hands where we can see them. Stand up slow."

There were three of them. Male. Two white and one black. The oldest was the speaker and he looked to be around eighteen.

They held small-caliber pistols, cheap, chromed little Saturday night specials. Inaccurate and unreliable weapons, but the .22-caliber automatics were still capable of taking anyone out at fifteen feet.

"You got food, old man?" The speaker had a sparsely stubbled foxy face, narrowed eyes and pinched mouth.

"No. Haven't eaten in three days. You got anything you can share with us?"

Laughter, hateful, venomous laughter, was the answer.

"We got something we can share with the little lady there," said the second boy, pushing a filthy baseball cap off his sloping forehead.

Jim was conscious of the weight of the Ruger Blackhawk Hunter in its holster, hidden under the coat. The realization came to him like a flash of lightning out of a clear summer sky. He was going to have to use the gun. If he didn't, then he and Carrie would be soon dead.

She'd take her dying a good while longer and slower than him.

"Little lady's got her period," said Carrie.

The black youth smiled broadly. "Most houses got more'n one door, lady," he said.

The leader of the trio grinned. "You're right, Michael, my man."

"Count ten, then faint," whispered Jim, taking care not to move his lips, confident that the crackling of the fire would cover the sound.

Out of the corner of his eye he saw her almost imperceptible nod of agreement.

"Might as well get to it," said the second of the group.

"Why not?"

"We got food," Jim blurted out, managing to sound guilty. He took a couple of nervous-looking steps to his left, distancing himself from Carrie. He flexed the fingers on his right hand, trying to ease some of the morning's stiffness from them.

"Shit! That don't make no fucking difference, old man, do it?"

Second Navigator Carrie Princip made a good job of it. She half screamed, hands flying to her face. The green eyes rolled back in their sockets, and she tottered sideways, away from Jim, before collapsing onto the dew-damp earth.

He didn't pause to admire her performance.

Half turning, instinctively making himself into a smaller target, he whipped the long-barreled .44 from its greased holster.

The three teenagers had all been distracted by the skinny blond woman's theatrical tumble.

The leader tried to draw a bead on Jim when he saw the big revolver appear in their victim's fist, but the timing was not on his side anymore.

The shot took him in the upper chest, the large-caliber, full-metal-jacket round punching a hole out of his back the size of a dinner plate.

The black youth began to turn away, dropping his own pistol, mouth open. Jim put the second bullet a little lower, smashing ribs and tearing the heart to pulsing tatters of torn muscle.

Both of them were still on their feet as he shot the third.

There was the lighter snap of the .22, overlaid by the thunderous boom of the Ruger. A spray of dirt furrowed near Jim's feet. But his shot had struck home, hitting the last of the murderous trio in the right shoulder, spinning him around, sending him staggering to his knees.

The black teenager had gone down like a steer under the poleax, falling stiff and still. The first one was still kicking and twitching, eyes wide, his feet moving as though he were trying to push himself into the earth.

The last of them looked at Jim. "Please, mister," he said. "Listen to me, mister."

"I don't have the time, son. You'd have killed us. You too shall die."

He leveled the revolver and squeezed the trigger a fourth time, blowing the top of the youth's head into shards of splintered bone and a pulp of blood-flecked brains.

Carrie was getting shakily to her feet, face white as parchment as she looked at the three corpses. They were all still, except for the leader's fingers, which were scratching in the mud as residual nerve impulses continued to operate.

Moments later even that finally stopped.

"You too shall die," she said. "By God, Jim, you sounded like some Old Testament avenging angel. Holding a smoking gun instead of a flaming sword."

Jim was reloading the Ruger as she spoke. "Yeah, guess I did," he replied.

He was relieved that she didn't ask him if it had really been necessary to kill all three of their attackers.

They left the corpses where they lay, but before moving on Jim searched them and examined the three dropped guns.

One was a cheap and corroded little automatic of anonymous make. Now that he could see them more clearly, Jim found the other two weapons weren't quite what he'd thought. The black teenager had been carrying an old Lorcin .25. Designed as a purse gun for women, it had been immensely popular toward the end of the twentieth century. Holding six rounds of .25-caliber ammunition, with a snub two-inch barrel, it had a smooth white stock and a satin chrome finish.

Carrie took it off him, weighing it in her hand. "Can I have this?"

"Nobody here to stop you. But you might do better with this Smith & Wesson revolver."

It was the 2060 Model, very similar to the old 650, which in turn was close to the Model 34 of nearly a hundred years earlier.

The weapon was a six-shot .22-caliber revolver with a four-inch barrel and a rounded butt, chromed steel, in nice condition. Twenty spare rounds for it were tucked into one of the pockets of the boy's plaid jacket.

"I like this better," she said, aiming at the dead trees around with the little Lorcin. "It's sort of neater."

"No," he said.

"Why not?"

"Twenty-five-caliber ammunition isn't all that common. Any bullets are going to be like pure gold these days. So, stick to a safer caliber like this Smith & Wesson .22."

"Can I have them both?"

Jim shook his head. "Take the revolver, Carrie, and get accustomed to it. Way things are looking, you might need to use it."

THE BUS HAD BEEN SITTING on a side road, its doors open, the key in the ignition.

Carrie had spotted the bright splash of ocher among the crimson foliage of a clump of dead sycamores.

They walked up a rutted trail, seeing the vehicle in a clearing. There was an elderly man sitting stooped by a narrow, trickling stream. As Jim and Carrie drew closer they saw that he was almost unbelievably thin and frail.

He looked up when they were within a dozen feet of him.

"Howdy, there," he said in a voice that struggled to get above a whisper.

"Hi." Jim couldn't think of anything sensible to say. From closer up it was obvious that the old man was close to death. The bones of his face looked as if they were ready to cut through the tight, blistered skin. The eyes had sunk back into the skull, and the toothless mouth sagged open. He was wearing a dark suit with a vest, a tie loosely knotted around the scraggy wattles of his throat.

"Come far?"

Carrie answered. "Nevada. Walked it."

"Good way."

"This your bus?" asked Jim Hilton.

"Name's Horace Korchik. Used to be the driver of old Betsy here. Came the troubles and I got her out the garage. Hid her. Me and the wife was going to use her to get out into the country. Come from Glendale. Wife died the day before we was leaving. Used to come picnic here in our younger days. Drove Betsy up with my wife lyin' snug on the back seat. Buried her about a week ago." His eyes narrowed. "Could be longer. Lost track of... Since then I just been waiting out here. Waiting to go join her."

The words came out in short, tired bursts.

Jim nodded. "I understand, sir. Makes a lot of sense to me. I'm back here trying to locate my wife and daughters."

"Where they at?"

"Over in Hollywood."

The head turned slowly, like a world-weary lizard, staring at Carrie. "She kin of yours?"

"Friend."

"Ways still to walk, mister.... Didn't sort of catch your name."

"Hilton. James Hilton. Commander in the United States space-exploration mission. Out of Stevenson Air Force Base."

"Carrie Princip. Lieutenant. Navigator. Good to meet you."

"Likewise. Forgive me not standing to greet a lady. Legs more or less gave out yesterday."

Jim looked at the school bus. "She fueled up, Mr. Korchik?"

Carrie touched him on the arm. "Jim," she said warningly.

The old man gave a feeble, cackling laugh. "Difference between a man and a woman, that. You want to take Betsy, don't you, Commander?"

"I'd appreciate it."

"You help me down to sit by the water…where I can see the grave. And you take her with my blessing." He coughed, his whole body shaking. "Course, you can take her without my blessing, and I couldn't do doodly to stop you. But you don't look like that kind of feller to me."

"It's a deal," said Jim.

They virtually had to carry the old man between them, setting him down gently on a patch of bare earth close to the stream. The pile of raw dirt was a few yards along to the right, vivid orange.

"Used to be long, green grass," said Horace. "Fact is we did our necking up here. Probably conceived our boy around this place."

"Where is your son?" asked Carrie.

"Chicago with his family. But Earthblood came. Difficult to talk on the phones. Said they had serious food problems. Last time we spoke, Karl was thinking of making a run for it. 'Screw the government' was his words."

There was a stillness, with the wind sighing through the dry branches.

"That was it?" asked Jim.

The old-timer nodded. "Never a word. From what we seen and heard, it could've been the National Guard. They shot plenty around L.A. here. Said they were looters and rioters."

"Were they?"

"No, lady. They was just a bunch of hungry people, doing the best they could."

Jim wandered over and stood by the grave, his head bowed. Then bent to stare and reached down with thumb and forefinger.

"What you found, Commander?"

"Blade of grass," he said. "Few shoots of fresh green grass."

"Yeah. Ironic, ain't it? I heard some talk of this. The plant cancer run its course. And old Nature's fighting back again. Just that it's too damn little and a whole lot too damn late."

"We have to go," Jim Hilton said. "Sure you don't want to come? We got food."

"Thanks, but no thanks. Here's the only place I want to be. And I don't reckon to be around here too much longer."

"Then wait," Carrie said suddenly, and disappeared into the bus. A minute later she emerged with a can, which she filled with water from the stream and deposited beside the old man. "No matter what, it's not good to be thirsty," she said gently.

"God bless . . . and go now."

Jim shook his hand. "So long, and good luck," he said quietly.

Carrie bent and kissed Horace Korchik on the cheek. He lifted a finger to touch the place, looking at the pearl of moisture. "Save your tears, little lady. Might need them later."

The engine started with a burst of gray smoke from the exhaust.

"He's waving to us," said Carrie.

"Wave back to the poor old bastard."

"No. Think he wants you to go over."

Jim was impatient to get going, but he put it back into neutral and walked quickly to Horace Korchik. "Yeah?"

"Where was it you said you was heading for, Commander?"

"Hollywood. Tahoe Drive, up there below the big sign. You know it?"

"No. Just that I recall having met up with a guy on a trail bike."

"When?"

He shook his head. "Time's... We had food well hid, kept us going. Growed our own. Had plenty frozen and pickled in the cellar. Mushrooms weren't affected by Earthblood. They... Oh, yeah. When? Around a month ago. Came from those parts."

"And?"

"He said they had a lot of bad sickness. All sorts. Plague and a raging immune-deficiency disease. And cholera. I recall he specially mentioned that they had cholera."

21

"Look what we got here. A nigger, all on his ownsome, with a big shiny truck."

Kyle deliberately didn't even turn around, managing to win the battle for self-control, even succeeding in keeping his voice light and steady. "Nigger with a big shiny truck that just ran out of gas."

"Niggers tell lies like bears shit in the woods. Figure I'll just take me a look for myself. Move a few steps to the side, boy."

Kyle took a chance and glanced behind him as he shuffled to his right, away from the cab. He was wondering when Steve Romero might make a move, and wondering just what the hell kind of move his friend might be able to make.

To his surprise, there was only one man standing there, holding a sawed-down scattergun, with a rifle slung over his shoulder.

He was just under average in height, skinny as a lath, with a gingery beard and deep-set eyes. His feet were tucked into enormous green rubber boots, and a long plastic raincoat drooped down below his knees.

It occurred to Kyle that the man, who looked in his late thirties, was probably mad.

"You look at me that sideways squinty way, boy, and you get to be one dead nigger real quick. You hear me?"

"Sure. Sorry. Shall I move a bit farther away from the truck?"

"Why not?" The voice belonged to someone from the South. Kyle had traveled below the Mason-Dixon line on a commission when he'd been a photographic journalist, with Leanne, just before they got engaged.

He hadn't thought about Leanne as much as he should have since the *Aquila* had fallen from the sky. It had been vaguely agreed that he and Steve would try to loop back south toward Albuquerque, in New Mexico, where she had been living, after checking out Steve's son, Sly, up in Aspen.

Nothing much had changed since he'd witnessed the South firsthand. Same good old boys drinking redneck beer in redneck bars under the Stars and Bars. Georgia rednecks and Alabama rednecks and the Mississippi rednecks. Oh, yeah, the Mississippi rednecks.

"I said to sit down, boy!"

"Sorry."

"You educated? Can tell you are, boy. One of those uppity Northern niggers. I killed three like you last week. Camping they were, eating good fresh deer meat. Real yummy, boy. Screwed the bitch first. Cut her throat open."

The little man was close to the cab, the twin muzzles of the scattergun gaping toward Kyle.

"Something just came to me, boy."

"What?"

"Why bother keeping you alive? Good question, that. Answer is, I'm not no more."

Steve was visible in the shadows of the cab, trying to wriggle silently around.

Kyle coughed. "Hey, listen, mister," he said, trying desperately to buy himself a few more moments of precious life.

"What?" the man asked unwillingly, curious and suspicious.

"I figure you're about as crazy as a shithouse rat, you pecker-wood piece of white trash."

The underslung jaw dropped open, and the little man stared at Kyle. "You say... Why, you stinkin' black bastard, I'm..."

Steve took the chance while the stranger's attention was distracted, sitting on the front seat, leveling a short-barreled pistol.

The shotgun was trembling with the man's rage, and Kyle stared into instant obliteration, waiting for Steve to shoot.

Nothing happened. "Do it, for Christ's sake!" Kyle yelled, terror pushing his voice way up the scale.

"I'm 'bout to," replied the little man, recovering some tattered vestiges of what probably passed for self-control.

"Steve!"

Finally Steve Romero broke himself out of the frozen grip of horror, leveled the gun a second time and pulled the trigger.

Still no result, but now the scattergun was swiveling around toward the cab of the Volvo.

"The safety fucking catch, Steve!" screamed Kyle Lynch.

At last the handgun fired, a thin, weak sound, muffled by the surrounding cab.

"Missed me, you shithead!!" yelped the man, pulling the trigger on the shotgun.

The shot erupted into the side of the truck, taking out the windshield and the driver's window on the far side.

Steve had been quick enough to throw himself backward, so that the starring burst of lead exploded over him.

Kyle realized that the noise had come from one of the twin barrels. He was torn between the desire to run away and the awareness that the man could now only kill one of them. And it was probably going to be the trapped Steve Romero.

Frantically he looked around. There were stones at his feet, mostly tiny pebbles, with the occasional fist-sized quartz-lined rock.

Kyle snatched one up and heaved it at the murderous stranger with a clumsy, round-arm throw, aiming at the man's head and missing him by at least six feet. The missile bounced off one of the front tires and landed in the dirt just in front of his feet.

"What the fuck?" He glanced around at Kyle, his lips peeled back off the rotten teeth in a wolfish snarl of hatred.

Steve sighted between his own feet and fired the automatic three more times, the gun bucking in his right hand.

One bullet missed Kyle by less than a yard. A second round plucked at the plastic raincoat, while the third bullet hit the little man in the face, close to his nose.

It knocked him sideways, the shotgun falling in the dirt, the impact firing the second barrel. He tottered a few stumbling steps, away from the truck, both hands pressed to his face. Bright scarlet blood was pouring between his fingers, patterning the dust around him.

Finally he sat down with a thump, moaning and cursing, ignoring the rifle still slung across his shoulders.

Kyle started toward him, then stopped, rocking on the balls of his feet, paralyzed by fear and indecision.

Steve crawled out of the cab and stood by the open door, the gun pointing at the dirt. His face was pale with shock.

"What shall we do?" he asked.

"Kill him," replied Kyle, "before he tries to take us out."

"Shoot him again?"

"Sure. For Christ's sake, Steve. He would have killed us."

"Oh, my sweet Lord, I'm done for, boys. I'm done for."

Blood was dappling the transparent coat, pooling over the spread thighs.

"Shoot him, Steve."

"I don't think... You do it, Kyle. I've done my bit. I shot him once. Now you shoot him and we're equal."

"This isn't some kind of school-yard game, Steve. He was going to send us both off to buy the farm."

Steve shook his head and lobbed the gun across. Kyle fumbled and nearly dropped it.

Now the little man on the ground was moving, struggling to disentangle the rifle from his shoulder.

With the hands busy and away from the face, Kyle could see the damage wrought by the bullet. It had gone in through the left cheek, directly behind the nose, and exited the other side, clawing out a chunk of flesh and bone, removing part of the upper jaw.

It was a ghastly wound, but Kyle could see that it wasn't likely to prove immediately fatal.

Gripping the gun so hard he wondered if he might be leaving finger marks impressed in the butt, Kyle stepped behind the seated man.

He stopped what he was doing and stared up. "Prefer it if your friend did it, nigger." The words were distorted by the bubbling crimson froth that tumbled over his neck and chest.

"Fuck you," said Kyle.

He leveled the gun at the nape of the man's neck and squeezed the trigger. It kicked so much that he nearly missed, even at the range of under four feet, the bullet barely clipping the side of the skull. But it was still enough to knock him over in the dirt, unconscious.

Kyle bent and kept firing the gun until the hammer clicked on an empty chamber. The stranger's head was pulped.

"Satisfied, Steve?" shouted Kyle. "Does that make us equal, friend?"

But that violent act, born of fear and disgust, had left the gun an empty threat.

Though they strip-searched the cab, there was no more ammunition for the empty automatic. Nothing of any use.

"It says on the side it's made by Mondadori in Italy and it fires .32-caliber bullets," said Steve. "Might as well take it with us. Least there's probably a chance of finding some ammo."

"Yeah, guess so. And we got this sawed-off shotgun. It's a 12-gauge, it says. There isn't any maker's name on it. Been filed off. But there's six rounds for it."

The rifle was a V Model Mannlicher, bolt-action, chambered for the .357 Magnum bullet with an 8-round magazine and a scope sight.

The dead man also had a knife at his belt, a honed bowie with a sixteen-inch blade. Steve took that, as well as the shotgun.

Kyle tucked the automatic into his belt and slung the Mannlicher over his shoulder.

"Let's go," he said.

They made good time, and by October 10 they'd managed to get very close to Aspen.

22

Jim put his foot slowly down on the brake, easing the school bus to a halt. He put the gearshift into neutral and pulled up on the hand brake, leaned on the wheel and stared out of the front windshield.

Carrie Princip had been dozing on the back seat and she came stumbling sleepily forward. "What is it, Jim?"

He simply pointed.

She closed her eyes and turned away, putting her hand over her mouth. Moved a few seats toward the rear of the school bus and sat down, head bowed.

There was a long rope strung clear across the blacktop, between two dead oak trees. Live oaks, noticed Jim, recognizing the irony of their name in this green-turned-red world.

Five corpses dangled from the rope, hung by the necks. The cable had stretched in the weather, and the middle three had their feet dragging on the surface of the road. The outside pair were just off the ground, bobbing and dancing in the light wind like hideous marionettes.

Like virtually all of the dead that Jim and Carrie had seen in their eight days away from Stevenson, these looked to have been dead for weeks, maybe even for months.

The eyes had gone, and the thin strands of windblown hair straggled off leathery skulls. None of the five wore even the most ragged remnants of clothing. Birds had done their work so well that it wasn't even possible to tell the sex of any of the bodies.

But there was a clue as to how and why they'd all died.

A broken door leaned up against the cracked trunk of one of the trees, with a message painted, surprisingly neatly, upon it: "They brought sickness so they were executed legally."

"Wonder what 'legally' means?" said Jim Hilton. "Sounds like we've encountered the first of some vigilante justice, Carrie."

"That old man Horace mentioned he'd heard they had some disease up this way, didn't he? Cholera was one."

"Yeah. We're not far from my home now. An hour or so if the roads are clear."

They'd made poor time in the bus, struggling on the narrow, tight bends, having to stop at frequent intervals to clear fallen trees and bushes off the highways.

Now evening was approaching again, with a fire-bright sun setting away beyond the distant Pacific Ocean.

A couple of miles back they'd crested a rise and glimpsed the water, glistening like a sheet of beaten silver. It was also possible to see a corner of the fabulous city of the angels, gridded out far below them.

Jim Hilton had stopped and climbed out, shading his eyes with his hand.

"My God, I've never seen the air so clear. I guess it's because there's no industry and no vehicle exhaust emissions. Like looking down through the finest diamond."

Now the western sky was tinted purple with strands of darker clouds.

"You going to cut the rope?"

He shook his head. "No. Reckon old Betsy can push her way through."

"I don't think I want to watch this," Carrie said. "But I guess you're right. Could just be part of a trick to get us outside."

He engaged first gear and let the yellow bus roll slowly forward until it touched the central trio of corpses.

He'd expected that the rope would probably have rotted away and would have snapped easily. But it tautened and held, stretched like a bowstring, against the power of the bus.

Two of the bodies were hoisted, their skeletal limbs pressed snugly to the safety glass, skulls rotating as though they were trying to find a way into the driver's cab.

"Cut it, Jim," called Carrie. "That's really a triple gross-out."

"It'll manage it. Come on, Betsy, show 'em what you can do."

He floored the pedal, the engine roaring. It was the tree on the right of the road that gave way, its dead roots losing the unequal struggle. The dead oak and the rope and the bodies vanished under the bus as it suddenly accelerated, then equally suddenly, jerked to a juddering, protesting halt.

Jim swore and put it back again into neutral, using the vacuum brakes.

"What's happened?"

"Rope's caught."

"Where?"

"Round the axle, I guess, or the brakes. Jammed some place."

He crawled underneath, finding that his worst fears were confirmed. There was a great knot of cable and splintered bones and tree, all tangled around the front axle on the right side.

"Hopeless," he said, dusting himself off. "It's hopeless."

"We walk?"

He shrugged. "Could be safer, seeing what happened to those hanged people... Means there might be patrols out. It's not far."

As he led the way across the steep hills, Jim remembered picnics with Lori and the twins. Hot summers with the plastic foam cooler and Cokes and pieces of chicken breast.

"It'll soon be dark."

"Yeah."

With the sun almost down, it was proving a rough scramble across the steep ravines of the dust-dry scrubland.

Somewhere near the old reservoir they both heard the distant ringing howl of a coyote.

"Must've been good times for creatures like that," said Carrie.

"Crows and coyotes. All the scavengers. Probably the rats and the cockroaches have taken over in the hearts of the big cities."

"Think we'll stay up here in the hills, Jim. Though, reckon we'll manage to reach your house tonight?"

"Could be. But it's going to be way on past midnight."

Using narrow paths, half-remembered, Jim Hilton took the woman close by the haunting, haunted shapes of the nine colossal letters that spelled out the name of Hollywood.

They shimmered white in the ghostly moonlight, towering high above them.

"Read someplace that a woman threw herself off the top of one of them," Carrie said, voice hushed. "Maybe hadn't made it in silvertown."

"Tinseltown. That was what they used to call it. Tinseltown."

TAHOE DRIVE SNAKED UP and around and in and out, overlooking the valley beneath and the distant black block of Los Angeles.

"Time was you'd have seen nothing but lights down there," said Jim.

Now it was grave silent.

The houses on both sides of the road were totally still.

"That was the Harknetts' place. Gave great parties. Vodka by the gallon. Friendliest people you ever met. Andy Wells lived there. Had one of the all-time great messy divorces. Talk about the wicked witch of the west. That . . . hey, it's been burned down. Shame. Tom and Zena Hedger. College folk. Could never master his barbecue, though. Generally finished up with a call to the fire service."

"How far to your place?"

"Couple of hundred yards, on the left. Just past that abandoned Subaru."

On an impulse, Jim drew the Ruger from its holster. The short hairs at the nape of his neck had begun to prickle.

"What you seen?" whispered Carrie, drawing her own six-shot revolver.

"Nothing. Just a feeling, but I learned to trust that when I've been backcountry. Up in Montana once, near Swiftcurrent Lake on a late-evening hike. Had the same feeling and when I walked around the next corner there was a sow grizzly with a cub."

"Hey."

"Know what steps I took?"

She smiled, teeth white in the gloom. "Yeah. Fucking long ones, Jim."

They stood still. Something rustled through the dead, cropped grass of his neighbour's lawn, making him start. There was a glimpse of a sinuous shape sliding toward the side of the plot.

It had been fairly common to see rattlers around Tahoe Drive, and he figured that the absence of humans would have brought more of them down from the barranca at the rear of the street.

Jim found it almost unbearably strange and painful to see his own home under these circumstances. He'd flown out into deep space before, though never for as long as this last mission. But in the past he'd always, always been met back at base by Lori and the girls. Then there'd been the time of debriefing and press conferences.

Only after all that was out of the way would he come home on leave to a great welcome from family and neighbours and friends.

"You got your keys?"

He'd been slipping away into the past, and Carrie's whisper made him jump.

"Yeah. Picked them up from my locker. Think we'll try around the back."

A dog barked not far away, answered by another and another. While driving the school bus Jim had glimpsed, or thought he'd glimpsed, a pack of dogs, all shapes and sizes, running together through a burned patch of scrub.

There was a thick-mesh wire fence, chest high, all around the property. Jim walked along the side of the house as quietly as he was able, conscious of his boots crunching through dead grass. There didn't seem any visible damage. No broken glass, and the shutters were in place across his daughters' bedroom window. The back door was locked.

He could now see the moonlight dancing off the water in the pool. The level was low, more than two feet below the top, and it was easy to make out bunches of leaves and a couple of larger branches floating in the sullen darkness.

There was a mesh screen over double glass doors, and Jim tugged gently at it. But it was bolted from the inside.

The kitchen and the rear entrance to the house was to the left, and he reached it in half a dozen short strides. Carrie was keeping close behind him.

"Watch the garden," he said.

The security lock turned easily and Jim pushed the door open.

He stepped into his home for the first time in two years and four weeks, shocked by the instant realization that he wasn't alone.

23

"Tenth."

"The date?"

"Right. Today's October 10. We still got five weeks to get all the way into the city and sort things out. Then hike south down to Calico for the fifteenth of the next month."

Jeff Thomas peered into the mirror, touching his broken nose. "No problem at all, Jed." He leaned closer, trying to angle the glass to catch the dawn light. "You reckon I look stupid?"

Jed Herne was doing his morning's exercises, attempting to loosen the night's tightness from his knees. "No. You might be stupid, but that nose doesn't make much difference."

The heavy bruising around the eyes, which had made the journalist look like a querulous owl, was almost gone and the deep gash across the face had healed up, leaving a jagged scar that seamed over the stubbled cheek.

They were in a third-floor apartment in a small residential block to the east of Stockton, California, just off Highway 88, close to the small township of Waterloo.

The door was locked, and the steel safety bolt was slid across.

In one corner of the neat, spare living room stood the two mountain bikes that had enabled Jed and Jeff to make such good progress north and west toward San Francisco.

Finding them had been a big break of sheer good fortune. Six nights earlier they'd encountered a small estate of expensive-looking houses, perched high in the foothills. It was immediately obvious that others had also thought that they looked expensive and had visited them.

Every door and most of the windows were broken, and anything worth stealing was gone. Five out of the block of nine had also been fired.

The most comfortable place to spend the night was the double garage of the end house, and Jed and Jeff had slept there.

Jed had woken first, stretching, looking out past the open door toward the opalescent light of early morning.

At his side there was the already familiar snuffling grunts of Jeff, his nocturnal breathing plagued by his damaged nose.

Jed had let his eyes wander upward.

"Holy shit!"

The scavengers had never lifted their rapacious gaze beyond the walls of the garage and had missed a pair of top-of-the-range mountain bikes. They were neatly slotted away in the shadows of the roof, custom-made Engessers. One gold and one a glittering silver.

There had also been puncture-repair outfits and two sets of spare tires and tubes. With tool kits and everything you might need.

Riding them with the heavy backpacks wasn't easy, but they both found that the bikes were vastly better than walking. They could work up to an average of close to a hundred miles a day on level highway. And San Francisco was drawing ever closer.

EVERY DAY THEY SAW more evidence of the horrors of a forced mass evacuation.

Now, months later, it wasn't possible to guess when the exodus from the coast had begun. But it was impossible to miss the dreadful mute evidence of the results of the catastrophe.

The closer Jed and Jeff cycled to their destination, the more grateful they were for having the off-road bicycles.

The main routes were soon impassable, blocked by hundreds upon hundreds of broken-down vehicles and trucks. Leaving them, the pair picked out a snaking route over obscure cutoffs and quiet, neglected blue highways.

Past the silent legions of the dead.

The desert scrub and slopes of the Sierras had all been tinted the palest of pinks, with the tops frosted by snow.

All that was missing from the beautiful landscape was living people.

They'd seen cats and dogs, including what looked ominously like a hunting pack of German shepherds on the far side of a fast-flowing river. Three times they'd seen bears and once a cougar loping across the track less than fifty yards in front of their wheels.

It turned to favor them with a slit-yellow, contemptuous stare.

"Doesn't take long for the land to go back to the creatures who owned it first," said Jeff.

"It would make a good article, if only there were any papers to write for."

Every now and again there'd been a solitary human, keeping well out of their way. They also came across two more townships with barricades on the access roads. One was protected by armed men and women. The other guarded a deserted settlement of withered corpses.

Only once did they see any larger groups of people, and that had been at a point where the freeway dipped down below the old narrow road they were pedaling along.

Jed braked to a halt, standing astride the Engesser, swatting flies away from his face. "Will you look at that, Jeff?"

"Reminds me of a squatters' township in some dirt-poor Fourth World country."

Smoke rose from several places among shacks built from scrapped vehicles. The smell of roasting meat came flirting its way toward the two men.

Fifteen or twenty ragged, filthy figures came slowly out into the sunlight to stare back at the invaders.

Most of them held makeshift weapons, spears made from metal railings and crude bows and arrows.

They stood in a sullen, close group, looking up at Jeff and Jed.

The two men didn't say anything to each other. In unison they simply turned, remounted their trail bikes and rode away.

It was Jeff Thomas who finally broke their silence seven or eight miles farther west. "I've seen the future," he said, his voice quiet above the humming of the tires. "And I have to tell you it doesn't work."

JED HAD BEEN RIGHT. The chaos was unbelievable.

Every road they came to was blocked by stalled and abandoned vehicles. Twice there'd been fires and hundreds of cars had been fused into a huge carbonized block of blackened metal, the heat of the fireball melting the highway itself.

It was a quiet, beautiful October morning, and the still air was filled with the dry, brittle smell of death.

The open ground on either side of the freeway was carpeted with corpses. Families lay together, embracing in death.

Glinting among the dried corpses was the now-familiar sight of empty pill bottles. Green-and-brown glass, shining in the water sunlight like so many discarded jewels. The last resort of the starving and desperate refugees who had finally taken control of their destiny, choosing the time and place of their own deaths.

The last freedom left to them.

Jed and Jeff found the sight and stink of mass death so insidious, even months after the event, that they took a different route toward the city. They cut around to the north of Mount Diablo, finding fewer holdups that way.

But they also discovered that the big San Andreas Fault had been at work. Over the years the fragile earthquake zone of central California had been increasingly active, with major jolts in both 2012 and 2027.

It was Jed who drew the short straw.

He was cycling a little ahead of his comrade, freewheeling down a steep, winding grade. Thoughts of caution and potential danger left him, with the exhilaration of the wind through his hair, the pavement unrolling beneath the wheels.

He took both feet off the pedals, head back, whooping at the top of his voice.

Leaning into the sharp curves, feeling the adrenaline rush of danger as the tires slithered on loose gravel, he was riding on the far edge of control.

He never even saw the section of road where the fault had worked its malign magic, turning a fifty-yard stretch into a corrugated washboard with jagged cracks and humps.

The bike left the ground, and he felt himself tumbling sideways. A moment of flying and then the impact. A grinding crash and a splintered vision . . . spinning sky and earth and sky and earth and earth.

He could hear the faint sound of a wheel spinning and, somewhere, a bird singing.

"Jed, you all right?"

"Think so. Down here."

"I hit that road section. Fucked my front wheel and bent the frame. I came off."

"Yeah, me too." Jed fell quiet, realizing that this was a foolish thing to say. "Guess you know that, Jeff."

"Saw you going for earth-break orbit. That was why I fell off. Lost concentration."

"Sorry. I'll try and come off in a different sort of way."

Now he could focus. He had fallen fifty feet down a steep slope, his bike only a yard away from him. As he looked at it, the wheel stopped spinning.

Jeff was standing above him, silhouetted against the skyline.

"Want a hand?"

"Yeah." He checked out his vulnerable knees and felt the hilt of the kitchen knife digging into his hip and reached around to shift it. They'd both taken good blades from the first unlooted house they slept in. Not much use against rifles, but better than nothing.

Jed's had a narrow blade with a serrated edge to it. Jeff had picked a long, broader knife, honed so sharp it almost sang.

It was a struggle to heave the bike up onto the buckled highway.

They stood together, Jeff shaking his head. "Mine's gone to buy the farm, Jed."

"Still if we're lucky we can pick up another one. We're close to tens of thousands of houses. They won't all have taken their bikes with them when they upped and ran."

"Yeah. Guess so. Least we both got away with a scratch and a bruise."

Jed nodded, straightening the front wheel on his machine.

The bullet came out of nowhere, ploughing a furrow in the pavement just to their left.

"Behind us," said Jeff, dropping to the ground, the bike tumbling beside him.

They were near the crest of a hill, with the road sloping down ahead of them. The shot had come from the rising ground at their backs.

"Look." Jed pointed ahead, where he'd spotted a dozen dark figures scrambling agilely across the pink scrubland toward the highway. Setting up to cut them off from that avenue of escape.

Another shot rang out, this time missing them by a wider margin.

Jed looked at Jeff, holding on to the saddle of his bike then at the other machine, wrecked and unridable in the dirt.

"It won't carry two of us."

Jeff nodded. "Not with both our packs. Not even without them." His voice was high and strained, the words tumbling over each other in their eagerness to escape from his mouth. "Won't say sorry, as I'm not, Jed."

"What?"

His head still whirling from the fall, Jed Herne found that life had suddenly become utterly, bizarrely inexplicable.

Jeff Thomas had slugged him one, followed by a searing blow to his ribs, making him actually stagger a few steps, his fingers losing hold on the golden Engesser. But it was all right because Jeff had grabbed the crossbar and was holding it.

Getting into the saddle.

Another shot rang out, this time closer, kicking dirt and grit into his face as he lay on the highway. But he didn't recall lying down.

"I'm down, Jeff," he said, wondering why his voice sounded so thin and far away. Like a cartoon voice. The thought made Jed smile.

He opened his eyes, surprised to see that Jeff and the golden bike were gone. There was a gleaming blur, down the hill, toward the west.

At least his knee wasn't hurting at all, but he was feeling cold. And he had a pain in his ribs, like a small fire lighting up.

There was the sound of feet running toward him and shouting. But Jed wasn't concerned. He was far more involved with the mystery of his own dying.

24

Henderson McGill and Peter Turner were also carrying knives.

Like Jeff and Jed, they'd taken them from an abandoned house, but they'd been luckier. In what looked like the bedroom of a teenage boy, with rock posters on the walls and skin magazines at the back of the closet, they came across a set of good-quality hunting knives.

Steel hilted, with tempered nine-inch blades, double-edged and needle pointed.

Both men had their weapons drawn as they walked cautiously along the main street of Hustonville. Pete's Kawasaki was propped on its stand outside a small grocery store. Mac's Norton was leaning against the wall of the Fluff 'n' Fold laundry next door.

"Think the sign was a trap?" said Pete.

"Paint was new, still sticky. And we need gas or we have to dump the bikes."

"Town's dead as Dead McDead of Deadsville." Pete looked round. "This could've been a hell of a good place once."

Hustonville looked as if it had been put together for a movie about a typical American small town. Single main drag, with a boardwalk, and a few side streets straggling off, with what must have been leafy sidewalks before the Earthblood virus struck. Now there were just irregular rows of dead tree trunks, bare white branches sticking jaggedly out at all angles.

There were half a dozen stores, and an ancient building that would once have been the local cinema. But it had enjoyed its own last picture show sixty or seventy years ago and had been most recently a carpet salesroom.

There was also Ed's gas station. Only two pumps. One for unleaded and one, a rare sight nowadays, for leaded gasoline.

The two men walked slowly and cautiously up and down the street, glancing along the intersections at the neat houses with picket fences and stone-dead gardens.

There was a light wind blowing. Ma's Diner had its window smashed in. On the far wall, above broken tables and chairs, a calendar was flapping, showing a faded view of Grand Rapids, Michigan. But all the dates had been torn off.

"What day is it, Pete?"

"Can't you remember?"

"No. You're the second pilot. Should be your responsibility."

"You're the astrophysicist, Mac."

"Right. Well, it's October 10."

"Sure?"

"Yup."

"If we're getting up to your folks', we gotta make some good time."

Mac nodded. "I know it, Pete." He spat in the street. "And we're getting short on the hi-concentrates. Have to find some food soon."

Pete hesitated, scuffing in the dust with the toe of his boot. "You sure you still want to try and make it north?"

"See my family, you mean?"

"Yeah."

Mac sighed. "Got to go. Way the world looks, I realize . . . no, I accept that the odds are they might be done for. But both Jeanne and Angel are tough ladies. If there's any way of making it through the bad times, then they'll have done it. And they'll know that if I made it . . . that I'd come and find them. Doesn't matter where or when, Pete. You understand that?''

"Sure."

"But if you want to cut back, head for Calico for November 15, then . . ."

Pete grinned. "Together we swim and alone we sink. Or some shit like that. Come on, let's look a bit harder for this mysterious gasoline."

The small Episcopalian church stood on the grandly named Forrest Avenue, in reality a tiny, snaking lane with a dozen poor frame houses on it. The mummified corpse of a little baby lay on its steps.

On a board by the church gate, weathered and torn, was a notice. The usual one, once a common sight outside a thousand churches across the land. A text from the Bible, intended to draw the reader's attention to a serious contemporary problem of society.

"Must've been the last one before the lemmings left for the high cliffs," said Pete, staring thoughtfully at it.

The warning was taken from the seventh chapter of Ecclesiastes, beginning with the first verse:

> The day of death is better than the day of birth. It is better to go to the house of mourning than to the house of feasting. For that is the end of all men and women. Sorrow is truly better than laughter. Better is the end of a thing, than the beginning thereof.

"Cheerful," said Mac.

They redoubled their steps, then sat down on the sidewalk by their bikes, neither of them speaking.

Mac was tossing a rounded sandstone pebble from hand to hand, whistling quietly to himself. Pete was cross-legged, palms flat on his thighs, in a version of the lotus position. His eyes were closed, and he hadn't spoken for fifteen minutes.

The voice came from above them. "You guys want some gas for them hogs? That why you stopped here in Hustonville?"

Pete didn't respond at all. Mac replied over his shoulder.

"You got some for sale, lady?"

"Maybe."

He was trying to judge the voice. Female, aged around fifty. Redneck kind of voice. Tough.

"All right if we turn around?"

The woman sounded surprised. "Course. Why not, mister. You got to look someone plumb in the face if'n you want to do a deal."

There were two women, standing on the rickety balcony above Ma's Diner. The one doing the speaking was closer to sixty. Gray hair under a swallow's-eye bandanna, thick glasses. The other was around twenty, also wearing spectacles. Short brown hair. Mac couldn't see from down in the street if either of them was carrying a gun.

"You got gas to sell?"

"Sell?"

"Sure." He fumbled in his jacket pocket for a fistful of dollars. Two hundred dollars in tens and fives from his locker at Stevenson Base. Pete was finally taking notice, starting to stand up, coming out of his meditation.

The younger woman said something, and the older one laughed.

"What's funny?" called Mac.

Pete's voice at his shoulder hardly even reached a whisper. "Two across the street. One in a hardware store, other in alley beyond."

The older woman answered him. "Daughter says we don't lack paper to wipe our asses, mister. Money don't buy happiness, my mother used to say. Now, after Earthblood, it doesn't buy you a damn thing. What else you got to trade?"

"Food?" called the younger one.

Mac glanced at Pete. The sharp eyes beyond the thick lenses didn't miss the movement.

"We're honest, mister. Two rifles trained on you across the way. We could easy have taken you both within two minutes of reaching town. Me and my three daughters. Laid you in the dirt."

"Why didn't you?" asked Pete.

"Not our way. That the way you two like to deal with folks?"

"No."

"Since Earthblood come out of the north like Sherman on his way to the coast, we seen plenty of folks at first—a real flood of them. Most died. We hid out at a place out in the hills. Had us plenty of food then. The flood became a summer trickle, then the trickle turned drought dry."

The daughter chimed in. "You the first in six days. Or seven?"

"We'll trade some hi-concentrate food in our packs for gas."

"Sure you will."

A third voice came from over the street. "They don't have guns, Ma. Unless they're hideaways. Checked them with the scope. Both got knives is all."

The mother clucked. "Big motorbikes and no guns. You boys come from Greengrass Halt, Stupid County? If we weren't honest, you'd be dead and we'd have the Kawasaki that needs plugs cleaning proper and that lovely old Norton, too."

"Can we deal?" shouted Mac. "We got us a long ways to go."

"Sure."

THE OLD WOMAN DROVE a hard bargain, but both Pete and McGill were painfully aware that they didn't have many cards in their hands. No guns, no cards.

One of the daughters, who had an empty, uncomprehending look on her face, stripped the Kawasaki while they bartered some of their remaining packs of food for gas. She kicked it into healthy roaring life after less than fifteen minutes with a set of wrenches.

"Good with her hands, Lucille. Lord gave her that and took other things."

"You aren't leaving us much, lady," said Mac. "Barely enough for another couple of days."

"You got gas, with the jerricans, to take you six or seven hundred miles on your way. You don't like it, then just ride on."

There was a smile on the craggy face, hardly touching the piercing blue eyes.

Pete grinned. "Wouldn't be that you're the 'Ma' from that diner, would it?"

"Yeah. That's why we got food stoked. Thought it'd run out in a month or so, but we've been careful. We got some tablets if it came to it. Like many poor folks ended up."

"You the only ones left in town, ma'am?" asked Mac politely.

"We are now. I lost my husband and son near the start. Folks thought we should share what we got. We didn't." She let the sentence hang, flat and ugly.

"But the dead didn't go to—" began Lucille, wiping her hands with a greasy rag.

Her mother slapped her across the face, fast as a striking cobra. "Keep that mouth shut, child," she snarled. She tried hard to readjust her smile and failed. "Kids." She shrugged.

"Yeah," Mac intoned, his fingers itching for the hilt of his hunting knife.

The trading over, the two men reloaded their packs and got ready to leave the fair town of Hustonville.

"Sure you don't want to stay?" asked Ma unexpectedly.

"Guess not." Henderson McGill shook his head very slowly.

"Four of us women and no men. You seem straight and clean."

"We are. But we got families."

"Hope you find them." Her handshake was dry and firm. "You seen green shoots coming through here and there. Maybe those of us who've got this far might make a good fresh start. Now that Mother Nature's had her joke on us. You change your mind, come back and look us up. Y'hear me?''

Though it was a cool day, Mac found he was perspiring heavily as they rode clear of the little township.

25

Though it was pitch-dark in the kitchen, Jim Hilton could see it clear as crystal in the center of his mind's eye.

The double sink was on his right, by the window that looked out across the pool, over beyond the reservoir, toward the hazy blur that was Los Angeles. The electric stove was beyond that, and then the day-to-day freezer, as Lori called it. The main chest freezer was out at the back of the three-car garage.

The index finger of his right hand was trembling on the trigger of the .44-caliber Ruger Blackhawk Hunter.

For a quivering, surreal moment, Jim was taken back to a night when he'd gotten out of bed at four, after a party with the Harknetts around. He'd been overcome with a desire to scrape out the dish of chocolate fudge sundae he knew was sitting snugly on the second shelf of their kitchen fridge.

He'd been sucking at the small silver apostle spoon that had been one of a set of wedding presents from his Aunt Elsie, savoring the rich sweetness, when he'd realized that he wasn't alone in the silent kitchen.

That time it had been Heather, blackmailing him into giving her half the sundae by threatening to tell Lori. Jim had been dieting back then, trying to shed a surplus couple of pounds.

Now he knew he wasn't alone in the silent kitchen.

On the step outside, Jim heard the faint sound of Carrie nervously shifting her feet.

"Lori?" he whispered. "That you, Lori?"

"Who that?"

The voice came from the open doorway into the hall. It seemed as if the speaker was crouching in the darkness.

"Who are you? And what the fuck are you doing in my house and where the fuck is my wife and my kids?"

It took a serious effort of will on Jim's part not to open fire at the invisible person less than fifteen feet away from him.

"That Captain Hilton?"

Now he recognized the accent and the slight lilt to the voice.

"Ramon?"

"Is me."

Jim relaxed a little, uncramping his finger from the trigger.

Ramon Hernandez had been the best handyman and gardener in the area. His plump wife, Maria, had been the finest hired cook, whose *huevos rancheros* could raise the dead and whose fabled *carne adovada*, with blue-corn tortillas, was the pride of every Hollywood dinner party.

"That really you, Captain Jim?"

"Yeah. Where's Lori? And the twins?"

The voice came from higher up, as if Ramon got up off the floor. "Not good news, Captain."

Those four words were like a stiletto of ice piercing Jim's heart. During the difficult trek to Tahoe Drive, he'd seen nothing but death and horror, but he'd clung to his hope that somehow things would be different back home.

"Can I come in?" whispered Carrie, hearing voices from inside the house.

For several heartbeats he didn't answer her. He'd heard her but he hadn't listened. She had to repeat the question.

"Oh, yeah. Come in." He holstered the revolver. "Ramon, can we sit down and talk?"

The voice drifted ahead of him, into the big living room with its long bookshelves and the stone logs in the fireplace. There was the scratching sound of a match being struck, followed by the flicker of light.

"We keep drapes drawn, Captain. Not many candles left now."

Carrie was at his heels, so close he could smell her sweat.

The single stump of candle gave only a quivering pool of light. Ramon was barely visible behind it, and the rest of the long room remained in deep shadow.

Jim perched his hip against the back of his own favorite armchair. He could just make out the pale shape that was Carrie Princip, standing by the picture window.

"Tell me, Ramon."

"You been in space?"

"Yeah."

"Now you back."

"So you see. Just tell me. We know something about this Earthblood that killed all the plants. Just tell me first where my wife and daughters are. That first, Ramon."

"My wife dead."

"Oh, I'm real sorry." But he wanted the man to hurry up.

"She was such a big...you know... woman." There was the shimmer of Ramon's hands describing the shape of his wife's hips in the still, dark room.

"Please," said Jim softly.

"Come see."

"Shall I come?" said Carrie.

"No," he said on a sigh. "No, just wait here for me, will you?"

"Sure."

Ramon had already gone out the other door into the corridor that led to the bedrooms. There was a time when Jim could have followed him, surefooted as a mountain goat. Not now. Twice he stumbled over furniture that shouldn't have been where it was.

"You all right there, Captain?"

"Yeah."

Now he could see another light. Another candle, steady and still, in what had been their bedroom.

Jim bumped his elbow against the corner of the door, nearly falling. His shoulder hit a picture on the wall.

A print of *Christina's World,* by Andrew Wyeth. He'd bought it as a present for his wife on their tenth anniversary, just before the *Aquila* had soared from the launching pad.

"In here. Keep hushed, Captain."

"Lori." He wasn't even sure whether he'd really whispered her name, or whether it had been whispered inside his mind.

"Is not Mrs. Hilton. Is Andrea."

Jim's eyes were adjusting to the faint light in the room, and he could make out a shape on the bed, lying still under their bright-patterned quilt.

"Andrea? Where's my wife? Where's Mrs. Hilton, Ramon? And Heather? I don't understand."

There didn't seem to be enough air in the silent bedroom. Jim swallowed, mouth dry.

"Andrea, baby," he called softly, moving until the bed touched his knees. He was aware of a foul smell hanging around him.

"I think you too late, Captain."

He spun round, reaching out and grabbing Ramon by the wrist, conscious of how thin and frail the gardener had become, the tiny bones feeling like a trembling sparrow in his fingers.

"What the fuck? Too late!"

"Please, you hurt me."

Jim let him go and knelt by the bed, his hand touching the figure beneath the covers. The smell of excrement and vomit was much stronger.

"Baby," he whispered.

"I think she has gone, Captain." Then Ramon leaned closer, his ear to the still figure's mouth. "Just barely there, but no help for it. Not long now . . ."

His daughter's arm rested on top of the quilt, and he touched it. Touched the shrunken fingers with his own.

"Oh, no. No, God."

"Cholera. Mrs. Hilton, she left about three weeks back."

"Left?"

"I bury her in the garden. Dig deep, Captain, so coyotes don't get her. Put big stones on top. Under magnolia. Think it might live again one day."

Tears were coursing over the stubble on Jim Hilton's cheeks as he held his daughter's hand in his.

"Where's Heather?" he whispered hoarsely.

"She gone only a couple days."

"You buried her, too, Ramon? By Christ, but you been busy for the family."

"No, not bury Miss Heather, Captain. She don't got the cholera. She couldn't stand it once her sister slipped into the long sleeping. She knew. Cared for Mrs. Hilton. Knew what was happening. Asked me to take care. She gone."

"Left. Where did she go?"

He felt the shrug rather than saw it. All Jim could see was the tiny, guttering candle flame, and all he could feel was his daughter's weightless hand resting in his.

The flame went out, and Ramon left him alone in the cold, velvet dark. Once he thought Carrie might have come in and sat with him.

Andrea Hilton died just after dawn, as the light shone through gaps in the drapes. At the very last he thought he might have felt a tiny response. A squeeze of her fingers against his own.

26

It seemed as if the whole of the Catskills had been wiped away in one catastrophic fire. A flaming holocaust that had swept clear across the millions of acres of dead and dying trees, taking away everything and everyone in its path.

Mac sat the saddle of the antique Norton motorbike, looking eastward, away toward the state line with Connecticut.

"Sixty miles or so, from the map. And then around another hundred to Mystic."

Pete Turner swung his legs over and off the pillion seat, stretching. "We've only got enough gas for another hour...hour and a half. Then we walk. Don't figure we'll get any gas around here."

The Kawasaki had finally given up the ghost the previous day, October 15.

On the way northward from near Memphis, the two friends had been lucky enough to find two small hoards of gasoline, both times in solitary houses set well back off side roads.

They'd increasingly discovered that the interstates and main highways were either blocked by abandoned vehicles or were the territory of roaming gangs of armed men.

The farther north and east they got, the worse the situation became.

When they'd set off from Stevenson base, three interminable weeks ago, Henderson McGill's intention had been to take the straightest, fastest route available. Stick to the interstates to New York, then up to Boston.

He'd quickly begun to have second thoughts.

In a single morning, not far from Lexington, Kentucky, they'd come under hostile fire from two of the killing gangs. The first time it was a ragged salvo from inaccurate hunting rifles. The second time it was a lethal spray of concentrated lead from three or more M-18s on full auto.

Mac and Pete had skidded around in a cloud of dust, taking to the shoulder of the road, the spray of dirt concealing them from any further bullets while they powered away on full revs.

Pete swore that the men who'd opened fire had all been wearing military uniforms.

Since then it had been side roads and extreme caution all the way.

They'd seen enough of the mountains of corpses on the outskirts of some of the small Southern cities to be able to make a horrified guess at what a metropolis like New York must resemble.

"Charnel house. Only people going to be alive in the big centers of population are ghouls and the clinically insane," Mac had said.

"You not going to Boston?"

"No. Not now."

"Mystic first stop?"

Mac had sighed, leaning back against the bole of a fallen tree, staring into the flames of the small fire they'd risked lighting. The temperature had dropped alarmingly as they moved north, with frost on the outside of the tents.

"Jeanne and the three oldest will have tried to get out before the going got too tough. I know them. And they'd have headed for Mystic to hole up with Angel and the four littlies.''

"Sure?''

''Course I'm not bastard sure, Pete! But it's the best guess I got....''

So then they'd reached the ebony wilderness of the Catskills, with one motorbike, its tank near empty, and a single day's supply of food, the last of the hi-concentrate. One tent and a sleeping bag each, a couple of good knives—and not much else.

Actually the gas in the tank of the trusty old Norton kept them going right across the state line into Connecticut before the engine coughed once and then finally fell silent.

''North of Danbury,'' said McGill, studying the creased remains of their road map. ''Near dusk. Could hole up for the night.''

''Some houses up there, on the right.'' Pete pointed ahead of them.

''Might be some gas stashed in one of the garages. I'll push the bike and you can carry the packs. That a deal?''

''Sure. Why not?'' Pete laughed. ''Few weeks ago I'd have spit in your eye at the thought of hiking around with a heavy backpack on. Now I guess I feel fitter than I have in years. And I've kept up the practice on the martial arts."

"Yeah. I've seen you, remember? Any son of a bitch tries to get cute with you is gonna end up with his head jammed up his ass."

THEY GOT LUCKY.

"Figure we're far enough away from any real big towns for refugees and looters to have got here. And we've stuck to back roads, as well. Seems like nobody reached these places."

"There was enough gas in that single can out in the garage to carry us the eighty miles or so to Mystic."

"If both your families are there, Mac, and they're all well, it's going to be a struggle to get nine more people on the pillion of the Norton."

The house they'd discovered had been owned by a realtor, a man in his fifties with a wife a couple years younger. They had no children but they'd owned a golden retriever called Helga.

Mac and Pete knew all of this because the house hadn't even been entered. Helga was lying in the bedroom, on the floor, with a crusted saucer by her nose. She'd been dead for months. The tiny round brass disk bearing her name was tarnished, stained with smears of green verdigris.

Her owners were also in the same room, side by side on the bed, their skeletal, sinewy hands clasped. The empty pill bottles were on the round table by the window.

Mac and Pete left the couple where they were. Their bodily fluids had leaked clean through the mattress, dripping and leaving a dark stain on the pale cream carpet.

Though death must have been all around them, the husband and wife had left a short suicide note, on the table, alongside the pills.

Food finished. No place to go. No point in going on. Poor Helga has gone ahead of us and we shall soon be joining her. If anyone reads this, do not cast a cruel, judging eye on us and what we've done. We are together as we've been through so many good married years. Horseman, pass by.

Mac pulled the door shut.

There was a single unopened tin of dog food in the empty, stripped-pine kitchen.

"Fancy it?" asked Pete.

"There's some catsup. Powdered chilies. Cumin and some oregano. Mix the whole lot up, and I reckon I could just about manage it."

They got a fire going in the grate, against the bitter cold that was riding down around them on the teeth of a raging blue norther.

The logs crackled, bright and dry.

"Guess there isn't any more green wood left anywhere in the country," said Mac.

"Maybe none in the world. Remember that all the tundra and forests across Russia had gone from green to red."

Neither of them heard a sound outside the isolated house.

The first clue that they had intruders was when the door of the living room swung silently back. Framed in the doorway were two figures. Both looked to be in their late teens, wearing plaid jackets and jeans.

Peter had discovered a supply of candles on a top shelf in the kitchen and had stuck them around the room on plates and saucers. In the wavering light the uninvited visitors looked like Halloween goblins. But

Mac had a feeling that the trick-or-treating might turn nasty and mean.

Mac's hand found its way toward the hilt of the knife in an instinctive reaction that vaguely surprised him.

The taller of the two spoke. He was holding a short-hafted ax. McGill noticed that the other one had some kind of device strapped to his right wrist, but he was in shadow and Mac couldn't make out what it was.

"Who the hell are you? You got any food? Any liquor? No guns? That your chopper out back in the garage?"

"Lot of questions, son." Mac stood up slowly, feeling a sense of vulpine threat seeping from the pair.

Pete also stood, flexing his fingers so that the knuckles cracked. "We got no food. No liquor. No guns. And the motorbike belongs to us. Now you got your answers and you can leave the same way you came in. Right?"

"Wrong."

"We're hungry, mister." The other intruder had a slight hesitation in his voice that wasn't quite a full-blown stammer. But it didn't make him seem mild-mannered or timid.

Pete took a step toward them. "We just ate a tin of dog food, squid. Only thing left in the whole house. Now get out. Before..."

"Before what?" He lifted the axe in a threatening gesture.

"Before I break you both across my knee. You understand me, kid?"

"Don't fucking call me 'kid,' you dripping old prick!"

"That's a good fire, m-mister. We're sort of cold, as well."

"Hell, let 'em stay, Pete," said Mac. "Where's the harm?"

"The harm is that they came in with their axe and...and whatever the other one's trying to hide behind his back. Come in here and try to threaten us and steal from us. Well, if they aren't out of here in five seconds, I'm going to forget all about my pacifist training and throw them clean through that window."

"You an' whose army, you old prick?"

Pete took three slow, hissing breaths. Clenching his fists and squaring his shoulders, placing one foot a little in front of the other, he adopted the classical martial-arts threatening posture.

Mac was impressed.

"Five seconds," said Pete.

The shorter one stepped farther into the room. He held out his right wrist, and Mac had a moment to realize that he was wearing a small gunmetal crossbow strapped to it.

There was a dull thunking sound, and something hissed through the air, followed by a strange, wet thud, like a hammer striking a side of beef.

Pete seemed to sag for a moment, as if he'd been kicked behind the knees. His hands went to his head, where he appeared to have sprouted a small, feathered horn.

"He's hit me with an arrow, Mac," he said quietly, wonderingly.

"Are you—" Henderson McGill stopped, realizing what an utterly stupid and pointless question it would be.

"He's...he's killed me, Mac. With a fucking arrow..."

Three pairs of eyes watched as Peter Turner's hands dropped away, hanging limply at his sides. His head half turned toward the door, the shadows playing over the stubby shaft of the crossbow quarrel that protruded from his temple. A worm of dark blood had begun to crawl out of the wound.

His legs gave way, and he folded onto the floor, his head striking the corner of a low table with a ferocious crack.

There was a rasp of breath, torn shuddering from somewhere deep within his chest. Then he was still.

Henderson McGill closed his eyes for a moment. So much had happened since the computers recalled them from the deep induced sleep on board the *Aquila*. So many deaths and horrors.

But this was different.

"This is personal," he said, hardly aware of having spoken out loud.

"No, it wasn't...." began the youth with the empty crossbow.

McGill closed with him and clamped both hands around his scrawny neck, using all of his enormous strength to hoist him clean off the dusty floor. His thumbs jammed under the chin, forcing the head back so that his popping eyes stared at the ceiling. His feet kicked and flailed, but Mac turned away, easily avoiding the blows.

"Let him g-go," stammered the other one, waving the ax in a jerky, frightened way.

"Sure," whispered Mac.

The snapping of the cervical vertebrae was startlingly loud, like a dry branch beneath an unwary heel in a hunter's wood.

The feet continued to twitch after the powerful man dropped the corpse onto the carpet to lie alongside Pete Turner.

"Not me, m-m-mister." The kid was backing away toward the door into the hall, the ax clattering on the floor. His hands were up, frantic. The stench of urine was strong in the room.

Mac snatched at the left hand of the terrified teenager and broke three fingers in a single vicious twist. The boy screamed at the top of his voice.

Mac smiled at him. A dreadful, cold smile.

"You sick little shit," he breathed.

He shook the still-screaming boy, then whacked him against the wall again and again. The body felt light and thin in his hands, and at last he felt disgust come over him. Disgust for what the world had become, for the murderous little bastard, and disgust with himself for becoming just like the rest.

Picking the boy up, he carried him to the door and flung him outside, letting him crumple in a barely moaning heap. "You be gone now," he said. "I find you here in half an hour, you'll be dead. Remember this, it's better to die decent than live like bloody ghouls."

The boy had managed to crawl off. Before leaving for Mystic the next morning, Mac set a fire, burning the body of his friend along with his killer.

27

The first few spots of rain dappled the top of the oak table set in the corner of the patio, near the angle of the stone walls. But then it began to pour down with a serious purpose and it layered the wood, slick like a sheet of ice.

A battery-operated digital clock-calendar was clicking busily away in the corner of the room. It was almost the only unbroken thing in the whole of the luxurious log-built house.

Steve Romero looked at it, hypnotized by the constantly changing numbers.

"Wonder why they didn't break that?" Kyle Lynch remarked, pulling the door shut, collar turned up against the sudden rain.

"Who needs to know what the time is? Or the date? Not now."

"I do," Kyle said, grinning. The empty Mondadori pistol was tucked in his belt, the

Mannlicher rifle propped in a corner of the ravaged room.

"You do?"

"Sure."

"Then I can tell you that it's eleven minutes after four in the afternoon of October 12."

"That mountain time, Steve? I mean, I need to know precisely what we're talking about here. Wouldn't want to miss my favorite soap by an hour because I was in the wrong zone."

"What's your favorite soap?"

The tall black navigator sniffed. "I guess... Yeah, Leanne and me used to watch 'Pity's Problems' most weeks. Always sick kids and dying grannies. Used to laugh till I cried."

"Well, it's mountain time."

"Sure, buddy?"

"We're three miles from Aspen, Colorado. In the heart of the Rockies. If this isn't mountain time, Kyle, then I don't know what the fuck is." He shook his head in mock disgust.

"Like you say, time doesn't matter much anymore, does it?"

"Want to know the ambient temperature? Clock shows that, as well."

"Why not?"

"In or out?"

Kyle threw back his head and laughed. "I don't... No, make it outside. Just been out there and it's cold enough to freeze the balls off a steel cougar. Close to snow."

Steve looked at the green digital figures. "There. It's one degree above freezing. So you guessed about right."

"Inside?"

It was Steve's turn to laugh. "It's one degree *below* freezing inside."

"What we need is a fire," Kyle suggested.

They found the cords of wood stacked neatly outside the back of the house, which sat high up the side of an isolated ski trail.

It didn't take long to get a good fire blazing in the wide hearth. They managed to block the worst of the gaps in the shattered windows with tacked-up lengths of torn carpeting.

"All we need now are some weenies and a bag of marshmallows."

"I'd settle for any kind of food." Steve glanced at himself. "I'm six-two and I used to weigh in around one-fifty-five. Alison said it was like getting laid by a xylophone. Now it's like a starving xylophone. I bet I'm way under one-forty now. Honestly can't remember the last real food."

"Jim Hilton used to call us the beanpole twins," said Kyle.

"Wonder where the old devil is now? Wonder how many of us will make it back to Calico next month?"

"I wouldn't shed floods of tears if Mr. Pompous gets wasted on the road."

"Jeff?"

Kyle nodded. "Right."

"He's not that bad."

"He's not that good."

"I wouldn't mind him."

"Really?"

"Yeah. Chicken-fried with duchess potatoes and a side salad."

KYLE DOZED in front of the blazing fire. Steve wandered through the house, eventually settling with an expensive shortwave radio. It had been kicked under one of the smashed beds, but it didn't seem too badly damaged. A drawer in the basement workshop offered some batteries.

He carried it back with him and sat down by the blazing logs, using their dancing golden light to examine the radio.

The sudden burst of crackling static jerked Kyle awake. "On duty right... Shit! I didn't know where I was. Thought I was back on the *Aquila.*"

"Nobody out there," Steve said, punching the small silver buttons to take it all around the dial.

"Wasn't that... Stop."

"What?"

"Take it back a little. Thought I heard a voice or something."

The hissing came and went, surging like invisible waves from the ether. Steve moved the controls more slowly and carefully.

The clock showed one minute past five in the afternoon.

Suddenly a faint voice emerged from the static. "Tempest on..." Then the background noise drowned out the voice.

"Find it again," said Kyle excitedly. "Find it, Steve."

"Shut up a minute. Using the fine seek-tuner control on it."

"Probably that madam from . . . Barstow, wasn't it? One we heard from space, raving on about Earthblood stuff."

"Ah, the green light's come on, showing someone's transmitting. But it's on bastardly low power."

"Tempest . . . anyone . . . teenth. On hour . . . ry hour . . . lice on fif. . . ."

Then it faded right away, and nothing Steve tried would bring it back again.

"Batteries are way down."

"Think that was Zelig?"

Steve laid the radio gently among the litter of household items. "Could've been. Could've been Wile E. Coyote for all I know."

"It surely—"

Kyle stopped speaking, his head swiveling toward the broken French windows that faced the snow-topped peaks to the west.

"Yeah," breathed Steve. "I heard it, too."

"Company?"

Both men crawled quickly across the room to grab their guns.

They waited in case the faint scratching sound was repeated.

"GOING TO CALL IT 'Jaguar,' I think," said Steve Romero.

"Jaguar?"

"Or 'Tiger,' maybe 'Puma.' That's the best name for it. No, 'Panther.' Yeah. Goes with its black color, doesn't it?"

The cat was surprisingly plump and well fed. It had walked confidently in when Kyle opened the broken glass doors onto the back garden. Making a distant mewing sound, it had picked its way through and around the piled rubbish on the floor with an incredible delicacy then sat calmly in front of the fire and started to groom itself.

It hadn't raised any objection when Steve knelt by it and started to stroke it. The head went back and the purring intensified. The slit green eyes narrowed with pleasure.

Now it was sitting on Steve's lap while he tried to think of good names for it.

"'Cannibal' would be good," offered Kyle.

"Why?"

"How'd you think it looks so sleek? Like they said about Alferd Packer when he'd eaten his hunting buddies. 'Him too fat.' Cannibal."

"Never. I'll call him 'Panther.' That's settled. All right?"

Kyle stood up and stretched. "No. I got a better idea. Give him here a moment."

Steve lifted the contented animal off his knee and let Kyle take it.

"What're you going to call him? This better be real good."

Kyle gently stroked the soft black fur, then held its head firmly in his right hand and gave it a swift, savage, sickening jerk, breaking the cat's neck, killing it instanteously.

"I'm going to call it 'food,'" he said.

Steve was shocked momentarily, but he couldn't argue the point. Without food, they'd have trouble going on. They both agreed that it was delicious and tasted remarkably like rabbit.

Next morning they set off to walk the last three miles of their odyssey into Aspen, where Steve Romero finally discovered what had happened to his ex-wife, Alison, and his eighteen-year-old son, Sly.

28

Jefferson Lee Thomas, once the superstud star journalist on the prestigious *West American,* was terrified. Frightened almost out of his wits and gibbering with panic.

His pulse was racing, the indrawn breath burning his throat. The palms of his hands were grazed and slippery with blood and sweat. His tongue felt like the bottom of a cowboy's boot.

While running through the burned-out ruins of the old Ghirardelli chocolate factory, he'd fallen several times, bruising his knee and knocking the breath out of his lungs. He had also cracked his broken nose again, bringing scalding tears of pain and a trickle of blood across his neck and chest.

Not far away, on the edge of Fisherman's Wharf, he could hear his pursuers.

There were about a dozen of them, though there hadn't been enough time for Jeff to take a careful body count.

Now he knelt beneath the gaping mouth of a shattered window, the fresh salt breeze coming in off the misty bay.

"Why'd I come? Why the fuck did I come here? Knew it was stupid. Don't care for the chick. Figured my place would be trashed. Nothing here. Why the fuck didn't I go with Jim? Dad'll be long dead. Thought I could find some place to start again. Now I'm fucking finished."

Outside there was an unearthly howling as the pack of hunters drew closer. Jeff shuddered. San Francisco in the middle of October could be a chill, bleak place. But he'd had plenty of friends. Where were they all now he needed them?

"Dead or gone," he whispered. "Probably dead *and* gone."

If only he'd used the stolen mountain bike. The *borrowed* mountain bike. Taken it and gone south on the side roads and narrow trails along the western flanks of the Sierras, heading out toward the meeting place in Calico on the fifteenth of next month. Where there should be company.

It was funny. The only thing that had been funny in the past couple of days. Not funny amusing. Funny peculiar.

The big white building shaped like a pyramid—what was it called? Didn't matter. It still stood there, soot streaked, amid the firestormed ruins of the central part of the city. On one wall, about eight floors from the point, someone had painted a message in bright red letters.

"1115CACA."

It had crossed his mind that it could be a runic reference to the date and place of the rumored meeting, a reminder aimed at those who might comprehend it. The fifteenth day of the eleventh month in Calico, California.

"For those who don't understand, no explanation is possible. If you do understand, then no explanation is necessary."

Jeff wondered where that old quotation had sprung from, and why he was trapped and hunted in the fabled city of fourteen hills.

"Fuck knows," he said, actually managing a weak grin at himself....

IT HAD PROVED impossible to get into San Francisco on any form of transport, even on the bike. Every single road was blocked solid with jammed vehicles. And so many dead!

Jeff had dumped the bike into a culvert, carrying on with his lightened pack, and his broad-bladed butcher's knife stuck in his belt. Hunger was becoming more and more insistent.

He'd eventually entered the city over the Oakland Bay Bridge, walking across the tops of the cars on the upper deck, picking his way in the dark, high above the racing water.

The idea of trying to get to his apartment, and even track down his girlfriend, was seeming more and more ridiculous.

The night wind had tugged at him, and a light mist had coated the rusting metal, making it slippery.

Jeff had reached over halfway, past Treasure Island, when a croaking voice from the shadows nearly made him fall.

"Would you have a can of beans, mister?"

"What?"

An old woman with straggly hair, wearing a thick coat several sizes too large for her, had waved a hand at him.

"Two cans of beans, mister, then? Or could you make it three cans?"

"Bugger off before I slit your throat, you stinking old harridan!"

"You have a nice day, too, mister." She'd raised her voice. "I can catch the scent of death on you, son!"

For a moment he'd considered pursuing her into the maze of trashed metal and glass to carry out his threat to open up her scrawny neck. But discretion had prevailed, and he'd simply continued on into the city, coming down off the bridge and walking cautiously toward the Embarcadero.

Among the shambles of ruined stores and smart eateries, Jeff had holed up until the dawn was well established. Then he'd crept warily out into the ruins of the city that he'd loved, the city that had been his home.

Somehow nothing stated the sad demise of the city as much as the bridge. The graceful arch across the chill gray waters, its girders painted a dark reddish brown. The color of the heart's blood of all the country singers who had come west and failed to make it. That was what his neighbor on Jackson Street, Mad Dave Caswell, had told Jeff the day he'd arrived in town.

Now, silhouetted against the pink sky, he'd seen that the bay bridge had a great gap at its center. Huge hawsers trailed into the water, and the middle span dangled in thin air. Much of it was stained a bitter ebony color, streaked with scorch marks.

Jeff's only conclusion was that there had been a massive traffic accident as tens of thousands tried to flee San Francisco toward the north, and there had been a fireball so intense it had actually destroyed the main structure of the bridge.

It was a sad and bitter sight.

Jeff Thomas had wandered the streets for a day and half, not wanting to go back to his apartment, guessing what he'd find.

It was a nightmare scenario from some futurist fantasy, but after a couple of hours, it all began to blur in his mind.

The overwhelming impression was one of fire. Building after building, block after block, reduced to tumbled heaps of charcoal and twisted metal.

Surprisingly there weren't as many bodies as the journalist had seen in much smaller towns. His only guess was that a lot of the inhabitants had fled into the countryside before death overtook them. Or had simply chosen to crawl beneath their blankets and fade away in their own homes.

But there had obviously been plenty of corpses around.

Otherwise, what were all the rats eating?

Apart from the huge gray-brown vermin that scurried everywhere, unfearing and oblivious to his passing, Jeff had seen comparatively few human scavengers. And those that he saw seemed eager to keep clear of him.

At the back of Walton Park, Jeff had found several blocks of houses that hadn't been damaged by fire. All of them had their doors broken and most of the windows shattered.

Hunger was setting its teeth into his stomach as he'd spent an entire afternoon laboriously picking his way through building after building. Most had been sucked clean by the scavengers.

But he had already learned to look in unlikely places. Kitchens were a waste of time, but cellars and utility rooms had sometimes been overlooked by the starving looters.

Just before evening on that day his patience had been rewarded.

It was a small bedroom, with posters of bronzed, muscular women in tight shorts on the walls. Maybe a teenage boy. The wardrobe had been stripped, and some of the drawers thrown onto the floor. But there was a long drawer beneath the narrow bed, almost hidden by a duvet.

"Bonanza!" Jeff had taken out a treasure trove. Trail food, packets of dried nuts and dates and raisins. Glucose and fructose tablets. Even some hi-cal drinks in cans and waxed packs. Mint cake in boxes.

He's stuffed it all into his pack, figuring he had enough to keep him going for at least a couple of weeks. Maybe longer, if he was careful with them.

Jeff had wondered about the lucky find. The interior of the apartment suggested that it had belonged to a middle-aged couple with a son away, probably at college. A son who hadn't returned home when the Earthblood disaster struck, and whose hidden hiking supplies had then been overlooked.

THE BLOOD from his nose was falling in great lumps, giving Jeff the illusion that his brain was dripping out through his nostrils.

His breathing had eased a little, but he still hadn't risked a look outside. The whooping and shouts had faded, and there seemed a chance that the hunters had lost his trail.

Ironically it had been the weight of the food in his backpack that brought lethal trouble to Jeff Thomas. He'd been walking through the deserted streets, with only the high, lonesome sound of circling gulls for company. Finally he'd decided to look up his own apartment on Jackson.

Several streets were blocked with the rubble of burned and fallen buildings, and Jeff constantly had to make detours.

He'd been close to the ruins of the Holiday Inn on Fisherman's Wharf, pausing to adjust the straps on the heavy pack, when the little boy appeared from some stunted laurel bushes.

He wore cutoff jeans and expensive basketball shoes. A sweater was loose across his shoulders, over a maroon sweatshirt emblazoned with an explicit hologram of a nude couple eating each other. The lad carried a baseball bat, the metal glinting in the pallid sunlight. He stood and stared at Jeff.

"What's in your pack?"

Jeff felt a pang of doubt.

He looked more carefully at the child, figuring him for around ten years old. His hair was long, the color of Kansas wheat. The eyes were blue, cold, icy blue. There was a short-hafted knife tucked into the Captain Sirocco belt and a silver whistle on a lanyard around his neck.

"Asked what's in the pack," he repeated.

"There's a bit ax to cut the noses off little boys who ask too many questions."

"It's food," the boy stated flatly, totally ignoring the clumsy attempt at humor—and threat.

"You hungry?"

"What sort of a stupid question's that?"

Jeff could feel the short hairs prickling at the base of his neck.

"If you like, I'll give you a packet of mint chocolate."

The boy's eyes looked at him with a strange, unafraid contempt.

"You got a pack just filled with food. How come we haven't seen you before, mister? You been in the city long?"

"Coupla days."

"That'd be it."

"Want this chocolate?" Now Jeff was beginning to feel the beginnings of anger. "Or you can just push off, kid."

Before Jeff could move, the boy had taken the whistle and blown a series of high, piercing blasts on it.

Jeff's broad-bladed knife slithered from its sheath, but the lad was way too quick. Darting back a few paces, mocking the man's clumsiness, he blew the whistle in another echoing triple shrill.

"Why not run, deadhead?" he said, beckoning to Jeff with ragged-nailed fingers.

In the stillness of the cemetery city, Jeff could hear feet pattering toward him from all directions—all directions except from toward the water.

The backpack making him awkward, Jeff Thomas had run for his life.

Now, in the upper depths of the Ghirardelli block, he stood up and peeked out of the window. There was nobody in sight.

Jeff turned, but the corner of the pack snagged on a shard of jagged glass, snapping it. There was a crash as it spun and landed on the sidewalk, three floors down.

"He's up there," screeched a triumphant voice. "Let's get him."

He heard them entering the old building, coming after him, and he drew his knife.

Jeff had seen them as they trailed him. He'd realized that in the forefront of a raggedy group of ten- and twelve-year-olds were young, rabid-looking males.

In the dusty gloom, he waited.

Jim Hilton buried his daughter Andrea, alongside his wife, Lori.

Ramon and Carrie had both offered to help, but he'd refused. "My little girl. My job. Last thing I'll ever do for her."

It was just after ten o'clock on a dull, overcast Los Angeles morning, with tatters of mist lying out across the city.

The magnolia had once been the pride of the garden, dripping with blossom, shading the bottom corner of the garden near where the land dropped away toward the reservoir.

Now it was a dried stump, the branches brittle as rice paper, the handful of dead leaves carrying the familiar pinkish tint. But as Jim stooped to lay his daughter's body on the earth, he noticed a few tiny green shoots near the bottom of the shrub.

He'd washed the frail, shrunken corpse using water that lay in the pool, wiping her with an infinite tenderness, then dressing her in a clean nightdress. Pink, with small yellow flowers, edged with white lace around the hem and across the bodice.

The hair was matted, and he'd brushed out the tangles, parting it and putting in a tortoiseshell clasp that had belonged to his great-grandmother.

Jim couldn't bear the thought of dirt falling on the still, placid face and he'd taken a sheet from the linen cupboard and wrapped her very carefully in it. He planted a last kiss on the cool cheek before covering her head.

He knelt to place the first handfuls of dusty earth in the grave, sprinkling them as gently as he could, the shrouded skull disappearing from sight. Then he stood and shoveled in the rest, working quickly, aware that Carrie was watching him from the open french windows at the back of the house.

She'd already packed for both of them so that they could get moving again.

Ramon Hernandez had gone to the spare bedroom, to lie down to rest. It was obvious to Jim that the old man was at the end of his own road. The death of his wife, Maria, had finished his own interest in living. He had only stayed in the house to keep an eye on the dying girl.

Now that task was finished he was ready for his final sleep.

Jim had tried to persuade him to accompany them south.

"No, but thank you, Captain. I lie here and soon go be with Maria."

"What if Heather comes back here?"

"You leave letter, Captain. Tell little lady where you gone."

Before being tugged out of hypersleep on board the *Aquila*, Jim Hilton would have found the scenario absurd. Utterly ridiculous and completely beyond his belief.

To bury his daughter in his garden, alongside his wife, while his other child had vanished into the Hollywood hinterland... and now to be ready to leave Ramon Hernandez to finish starving to death, alone in the spare bedroom...

"No," he said, closing his eyes, hands clasped in front of him.

Lori would have wanted him to say a prayer. She'd been born and raised as an Episcopalian, though living high on Tahoe Drive had relaxed some of her beliefs.

Jim cleared his throat. His voice hardly reached his own ears.

"Lord, this is my daughter Andrea. I was away from her for a long while and I missed a lot of good things. Least I was here at the closing of the day. Don't know what would have become of her if she'd had the chance to grow up tall. Now we'll never know."

He began to cry.

Silent tears were running across his cheeks. He'd managed to shave before beginning the burial, and change his clothes. His pants were loose around the waist and hips.

"And now she's sleeping alongside my wife, Lori. Can't pretend we didn't have ups and downs. Most couples do. But we had a lot of laughter together. And they're here together. Keeping an eye on each other. Telling each other secrets."

He heard a faint rustling in the dead undergrowth behind him, beyond the wire fence.

"Got to go now, Lord. Wish my other little girl was here, Heather. Understand why she couldn't stay any longer. Somebody said something about mankind not being able to stand too much suffering. Just wish, wish I could . . .''

Jim dropped to his knees, by the two mounds of earth, his hands to his face, sobbing uncontrollably, all of the horror and tensions of the past month flooding from him.

There was the lightest touch on his shoulder, and a soft voice, choked with emotion.

"I'm back, Daddy. It's Heather. I've come back to you."

30

The group of grinning, chattering boys had tracked Jeff down, scampering through the echoing vault toward him. They were calling out to each other, giggling and whooping as though they were on a church egg hunt on an Easter Sunday. They served as beaters to flush out the game while the older males were ready to move in for the kill.

He'd found a corner near a window, in what had once been a tofu eatery, put his pack on the glass-strewn floor behind him and gripped his knife in his right hand.

Now the older ones moved to hem him in, sinewy and menacing looking. They slipped around him, their knives poking at the air, toward his face and his groin.

Every face was cast from the same streetwise mould, with slitted eyes and feral grins.

"Come on, shithead," beckoned one.

"Walk away from the pack and you stay breathing. Do it!"

"Drop the blade 'fore you cut yourself with it."

Oddly all of Jeff's terror had left him. His pulse was still racing, but now it was the pure adrenaline rush of excitement. He knew that sheer weight of numbers would eventually take him down, but he was also determined to take some of the bloodthirsty little jackals with him.

Several of them had bizarre kinds of jewelry. One wore laser baseball badges that sparkled and flashed in the semidarkness. Another, redheaded, had a string of part-inflated condoms, in iridescent colors, strung around his waist. A third, tall and muscular with a scruffy sort of beard, sported a necklace made from bleached fingerbones.

All of them kept laughing, making Jeff wonder if they were floating high on some secret hoard of uncut jolt.

"Come on," he whispered, remembering to hold the knife point upward. Years ago he'd done a feature on street survival among the gangs of Corte Madera, north of San

Francisco. A skinny Latino girl had given him a crash course in how to stay alive with a sharpened blade.

"Come on," he breathed, wanting now to get it all over with. Finish it now. Their blood and his.

Then another voice, raised but cold and detached, cut through the jabbering taunts, taking everybody by surprise.

"First one to make a threatening move gets to be exceedingly deceased."

Everyone looked over toward the doorway that led to the main staircase.

The woman was white, with neatly trimmed gray hair, in a khaki trouser suit, the pants legs tucked into combat boots. She had a small backpack on, with a scoped rifle slung over her shoulder. Jeff's first guess put her in her late fifties. She was tall, close to six feet.

She was holding a 16-round, 9mm Port Royale machine pistol.

She had an amazing presence, both calm and intensely threatening at the same time. It held Jeff where he was and froze the gang of juvenile killers.

"Everyone can put their blades down on the floor, slow and easy."

"You gonna chill us all out, lady?" said the red-haired boy.

"If I have to. Just a coupla questions first. Get the right answers...and I'm out of here and you can all carry on with your sporting games."

"They're going to murder me," said Jeff, aware his voice had risen to a nervous squeak.

"Course they are. You probably got some looted food in your pack. They want it. Taking you out's their easiest option."

"You shouldn't push your fuckin' nose in our business, old woman," said the tall one wearing the necklace of fingerbones.

The gun made surprisingly little sound.

A small neat hole appeared between his eyes, and the impact kicked him backward. His legs turned to wet string, and he folded onto the floor. The concrete wall behind was stippled with a mixture of bone and blood and brains and matted hair.

"Let's get these knives down, shall we?"

There was a faint tinkling sound of steel against stone as everyone, including Jeff, stooped and did as the woman had said.

"Now. A question and I'll be on my way. Let you get on."

"Come on," began Jeff, hesitating as the nuzzle of the Port Royale swung an inch or two in his direction. "You can't let them do this."

"Oh, but I can, Mr...? I don't believe I've had the pleasure of your acquaintance?"

"Thomas. Jeff Thomas. I'm a journalist, I used to be a..."

The woman lifted the index finger of her left hand. "From the *West American?* Went off a couple of years ago on the...what was it called? The *Aquila?* That was it. And now you're back again. I have to admit that I could, just possibly, find that passably interesting."

One of the boys shuffled his feet, catching a steely glance from the light blue eyes.

"Landed the twenty-fifth of September, Mrs....? Could I know your name?"

"Simms. Nanci Simms. Now, you being who you are intrigues me. Get this one right, and you might even get to live in this new paradise a while longer. Understand?''

Jeff started to sputter about bloody poor timing for riddles, but one look from her silenced him, and he nodded.

''Operation Tempest.''

''Yeah?''

''Heard of it?''

''Maybe.''

The thin lips tightened into a carbon-steel line. ''Don't condescend to play games with me, Thomas. I hold your life balanced on my index finger. Life or death is nothing.

''You see,'' she continued, ''in this post-Earthblood world of ours, life is the cheapest thing around.''

''Let us go, ma'am?'' said the redhead.

''A moment more of your time,'' she said, looking at Jeff Thomas. ''Tempest. And General John Kennedy Zelig?''

''I know something about him.''

A nod of the head. ''Good. There is a meeting place, is there not?''

''Yeah.''

''You probably know that there are two sorts of people interested in the project?''

''Not really.''

"Oh," she said with a note in the voice that indicated that she thought Jeff was telling a lie but wasn't that bothered about it.

"But I know about the meeting place."

"Ah, now that I would like to hear. Tell me where and when."

"No."

"No?" Something crossed her face that would have been a smile if it had come within a hundred miles of her eyes. "Because you think I might then simply walk away and leave you to these degenerates?"

"Possibly. Only way to find out if I'm speaking the truth is for you to come with me. To the place I tell you about."

Nanci Simms stared at him. "I never met a journalist who wasn't a mindless, voracious and stupid piece of ordure. Perhaps you're an exception. At least you don't seem stupid."

"If you save me, I'll show you where to go. And I'll come with you, all the way."

This time the smile reached the eyes. "Well, I'm certain I'll feel immeasurably safer for having you along, Jeff."

"Can I pick up my knife and my pack?"

"Sure thing," she said, waving the machine pistol in a warning gesture. "But take care not to get yourself between them and this."

"Please..." moaned one of the boys, dropping to his knees in the broken glass, face as white as wind-washed bone.

She leveled the neat black pistol at him, not betraying any emotion.

"Listen to me, you gutter scum," she said briskly. "This gentleman and I will shortly be departing from the Ghirardelli building. Before we go, I want all those knives thrown out of that window. Then you will remain here and count to ten thousand, quite slowly. After that I will remove any of you I might chance to see again."

Nanci Simms pointed at the boy with the waistband of colorful condoms. "Throw away the blades."

Jeff was now between the woman and the door, and it crossed his mind to make a run for it and get away from the blood-eyed old crazy. But he couldn't shake off the uneasy feeling that she would probably prove able to run much faster than him.

"Good decision, Jeff," she said over her shoulder. "Would've been dead before you reached the stairs if you'd tried for it."

NANCI TOPPED HIM by four inches, striding through the deserted streets of the city with a long, rangy step. The steel-tipped heels of her polished boots rang in the silence.

She'd asked him if he had any place to stay for a night. She rubbed a ruminative finger along the side of her nose when he mentioned his apartment on Jackson Street.

"Might be undamaged. Let's go see."

When they reached his apartment, they found the door kicked in, but there was little serious harm. The looters had been through the kitchen and took anything that could possibly be eaten, as well as all the knives. But they hadn't stayed to trash the place.

Nanci was sprawled out on the sofa, legs crossed. She'd refused any of the trail food, pulling some jerky from her own, much smaller pack. Jeff had nibbled on a fruit-and-oats bar, finding he didn't feel as hungry as he thought he would.

He stood by the side table under the window, where he'd laid out one of his Civil

War battle tableaux using the miniature models that he'd cast and painted himself. To his amazement, the tiny soldiers still stood, unharmed, among the rolling hills of dark green cardboard.

Nanci had glanced at it as she prowled around the apartment, and now she got up and sauntered over.

"Antietam," she said, softly.

Jeff was flabbergasted. "How the sweet fuck do you know that?"

"Majored in History. The War between the States was my last-year dissertation." She looked out of the window into the darkening sky. "September 17 of '62. Bloodiest day of the whole war." Her finger traced a pale yellow line on the diorama. "Hagerstown Turnpike. That's Dunker Church, I guess." A straggling, thin blue smear. "Antietam Creek. Burnsie's Bridge. Toombs up here with his Georgians, amongst the thick trees. Heavily outnumbered." She indicated a rounded incline. "Cemetery Hill. And Jeb Stuart away on Nicodemus Hill. It's nice, Jeff, very nice indeed."

He faced her, wanting to change the subject to what really interested him. "We go south tomorrow?"

"Right."

"How?"

She smiled, looking suddenly younger. "Jeff... I could walk it from here to Calico easily in the time we have. A whole month. But I prefer to travel with a modicum of style."

"First-class?"

"Absolutely. And if we find adequate transport, we can discuss the entire Civil War as we motor our way gently along toward this ghost town of yours. It'll be admirable."

"Transport, Nanci?"

"Let me do the worrying, Jeff."

Some distance away they both heard a sudden piercing scream, cut off as quickly as it started. It was impossible to tell whether it had come from a man or a woman. Or a child. Neither of them took any notice.

"Can I ask you something, Nanci, since we're going to be traveling together?"

"Why am I interested in Zelig and how did I know about Tempest?"

"And who the hell you are and what the hell you do."

"You believe schoolteacher?"

"No."

"Well, that's partly what I was. Rest of the time I was an assassin for Central Intelligence." She stretched lazily and cast him an amused glance. "Now I'm for bed."

Jeff watched her, unable to decide whether she was joking or not about her job.

31

It was a bitingly cold fall morning, with the previous day's norther veering to a ferocious easterly, dropping the wind-chill factor close to thirty below zero.

There were periods of hail, pattering off Mac's face, stinging the skin. Every hour or so the sky would darken to the color of tarnished pewter and it would tip snow across New England.

The Norton kept going, reliable as ever, though Mac had to slow it down to less than ten miles per hour on the patches of sheet ice.

It seemed as if he'd never finish the journey to Mystic. His hands and feet felt frozen, and he began to have serious worries about getting frostbitten.

His endless travels from the warmth of the Nevada desert to this bitter wilderness were beginning to seem more and more pointless.

It was as though there'd been nothing but pain and death from the first traumatic moments of their reawakening. As he rode on endlessly, the cold and the monotony amplified his fears that nothing good awaited him, either.

Unbelievably it grew colder and darker.

The headlight on the old Norton barely penetrated the driving snow that rolled across the blacktop in front of him.

Mac dropped his speed to walking pace, keeping both feet down, toes scraping along the glassy surface of the highway. Several times he had to swerve around tangled vehicles, many of them burned-out, blackened shells.

Once something darted from the blizzard, right in front of him, making him drop the bike with a jarring crash. There was the momentary flash of vast bulk and towering horns. His nostrils filled with rank, bitter scent.

The moose, or whatever it had been, vanished as quickly as it had appeared, and he hauled the bike upright and moved slowly eastward through the numbing cold.

When he saw the sign, it seemed like something out of a dream, and he stared at it uncomprehendingly.

Mystic—Home of the Historic Seaport.

Pocked with bullet holes, the sign was leaning drunkenly to the left, a battered remnant from a different world.

The bike was beginning to cough, struggling under the wintery conditions. He blinked, then said slowly, barely getting out the word, "Melville Avenue. One hundred and eight. One zero eight, Melville."

His lips were blue and his teeth wouldn't stop chattering. The Norton was meandering from side to side, the back wheel barely retaining any purchase. Mac could see a tremulous vision of the house and where it was, locked into his memory. But in the whiteout conditions nothing made any sense.

Nothing was making . . . sense.

THE LEAVES WERE fire tipped, running a whole range of colors. Green shaded into gold into orange—the bright tints of death.

It was a wonderfully balmy afternoon in late fall, with the sun beginning its slow decline. The water was tumbling in gentle white foam over lichen-coated boulders, down into dark pools.

All seven of Henderson's children were playing happily together. He lay back on the soft turf and named them on his fingers, from the oldest through to the youngest.

"John, twenty. Paul, eighteen. Pamela, seventeen. Helen, nine. Jocelyn, seven. Jack, six. And little Sukie, just four."

His first wife, Jeanne, lay on his right, wearing a skinny T-shirt in dappled colors of red and yellow. Though she was a couple of years past forty, she'd kept her figure well.

Angel, his current wife, lay on the other side, nibbling on a chicken leg. A can of beer stood open on a flat rock at her elbow, and beyond that was all the detritus of the big family party.

"We've done well," she said, following his eyes, down to the river, rubbing her hand through her tangled blond hair.

"Yeah."

The water was frothing, white . . . as snow as ice as ivory . . . as parchment—as death.

MAC KNEW that he was on Melville Avenue.

The white frame houses, with balconies

and turrets in the best Victorian Gothic style *looked* like houses on Melville Avenue.

The dead trees and bushes were weighed down with fresh-fallen snow, their pink color almost buried in whiteness.

The Norton wasn't there anymore.

Mac shook his head, puzzled.

He had a vague impression, an image in his mind of a tumble, a sliding into the ditch, as if he'd been a spectator and it had happened to someone else.

"Did I?" he said, unable to catch the sound of his own whispering voice.

Now he was walking, the heavy pack dragging in the snow that rose to his ankles, leaving a meandering furrow up the side street.

The children were laughing, their voices blending and merging until they began to sound like the banshee howling of the blizzard wind.

There was ice up his nostrils, uncomfortable. His feet didn't belong to him, nor did his hands. The cold had whipped the skin raw across his cheeks, and his eyes kept watering.

Watering and freezing, freezing and nearly closing, closing for good, maybe.

HE HEARD VOICES chattering around him, but Mac wasn't sure if he was dreaming. If he opened his eyes he could find out, but that would involve a huge effort and he wasn't quite ready for that.

Not yet.

"Lost a lot of weight." It was a woman's voice.

"Fit, though. Losing weight hasn't made any difference to some parts of him, though...."

That prompted laughter. Two women.

There was a gap while he slept.

"Knew he couldn't...walked. Paul and John backtracked and found the motor-bike."

"...hour and the snow would've buried it. Never thought we'd ever..."

A little girl spoke close to his ear. "Time to wake up, Daddy."

"I know, Sukie. Any minute now." Henderson McGill realized that he was home.

IT TOOK HIM four days to claw his way back to something like reasonable health.

His fingers and toes began to heal, though he lost most of his nails, blackened and dead. His sight was blurred by the cold and the whiteout, but that recovered on the second day, enabling him to see his family.

It had been two years, plus a few weeks.

Sukie had changed most. From a tiny child, barely toddling, she'd become an active little girl, rushing around the big fortress-house at a hundred miles per hour, a hundred questions in her wake.

The others had all grown in proportion.

John was now a strapping man, bearded, as was Paul, both with their father's muscular build. Pamela had shifted from girl to woman, with Jeanne's dark hair and coloring and solemn brown eyes.

There was so much catching up, and Mac didn't feel ready for it. Not immediately. Not until after supper on the fourth day. It was eleven o'clock, and the children had left him sitting by the fire with his two wives.

There was a snifter of brandy at his elbow. Beyond the reinforced shutters that covered the barred window the wind howled and the snow piled higher. The guns stood ready in every room.

But McGill felt safe.

"Now," he said. "Now I want to hear all about it. How come everyone's lived through Earthblood and how you got food and all."

The women looked at each other, both smiling. Angel answered.

"Long story, Mac. But I guess we have the time for it."

32

It was also snowing up in Colorado.

Fine and powdery snow filled in the hollows of the Rockies and spilled down into the valleys, drifting in the driving wind, piling against the flanks of the houses on the edges of Aspen. The white stuff formed a soft barrier across what had once been state Highway 82.

Kyle stopped and looked through the curtain of whiteness. "Wish I had my grandfather's old Leica camera with me."

"Arty-farty photographs of the grandeur of nature," Steve said with a grin.

"There speaks the one-time veggie and practitioner of transcendental meditation. The man with a sawed-off 12 gauge at his hip, a sixteen-inch bowie knife in his belt and a dozen rabbit corpses dotting the land between here and Stevenson base."

Steve nodded. "You got an ace on the line there, Kyle. Man changes. Have to. Try and live as a strict vegetarian after Earthblood and you die quicker rather than slower."

"Best get moving before this snow starts blocking the trails. How far?"

"To the last address I had for Sly?"

"Yeah."

"Another mile and a quarter."

They found the sign a quarter mile farther into the township.

Here, too, the sign prepared them, showing a world with a changed face. Aspen. Keep Out If You Don't Belong. Death For Strangers.

"Friendliest little place in the west," said Steve Romero.

The warning sign offered the threat of vigilante patrols. Kyle and Steve had already witnessed that all too often, particularly around the smaller towns. Fortunately the weather was sufficiently bad to keep the gun carriers indoors.

"Alison's place is along here. Overlook Avenue. Lot of new houses. Lives up here with Sly and her new man."

Kyle stopped and brushed snow from his stubbled beard. "What's he do?"

"Who?"

"Alison's husband."

"Not a lot. You want to know?"

"Yeah. You've never really talked about your family. All the years I've known you. I know she's married twice after you. You feel bitter. And your kid... Sly. All I know about him is that he's eighteen."

Steve coughed. "This bastard snow gets in everywhere."

"What does Sly do? What school is he at? Sorry, I mean what school *was* he at?"

"It doesn't matter. I don't talk about my family. About Sly. I just want to find him and maybe bring him with us."

"Alison's husband?"

"Name's Randy." He laughed bitterly. "Met him once, and he's just what you'd expect. Built like a brick shit-house with brains to match. He runs a ski-lift operation on the far side of Aspen."

"What if Sly wants to come and they want him to stay? You thought that one through, Steve?"

"I'll just take him."

Kyle slapped him on the back. "Look, the kid's eighteen. Got a mind of his own, right?"

"Sure, sure. Let's get on and cut the talk. I'm frozen."

When they stopped before a house, Kyle looked at Steve questioningly. "This it?"

"Yeah."

"Looks like something out of a child's fairy story. All that snow and the fancy woodwork."

"Wicked witch's castle maybe," said Steve with sudden bitterness.

"How do we play this?"

"Just walk in," offered Steve, patting the walnut stock of the shotgun.

"Want me to go around the back . . . get ready to give you a little support if you want it? Or, if you need it. . . ."

"I guess so, Kyle. I'll give you two minutes. Then you give me five minutes. If you haven't heard anything, just come running."

KYLE STOOD in the back garden, the snow falling about him in the infinite stillness. The world had closed in, and visibility was no more than thirty paces. No other buildings could be seen. There were lights on in the house, though it was still well short of noon, but the windows were steamed up and he couldn't make out any details.

He could smell wreathing wood smoke, with an undercurrent of cooking food. Baking bread, was his guess.

One surprise was the number of children's toys scattered around, some barely visible beneath hillocks of fresh snow. Steve hadn't mentioned Alison or Randy having any other, younger kids.

Kyle took off his pack and laid it under cover, by an elegant verandah that ran the length of the building. He eased the Mannlicher Model V rifle from his shoulder, checking that there was a .357 round in the chamber, remembering to make sure the safety was off.

Kyle Lynch closed his eyes for a few moments, trying to steady his breathing. Executing the redneck had been a hideous shock. This was different. In the next few minutes he might find himself having to use the weapon against more human beings. Maybe against a woman.

He checked his wristwatch.

Surprisingly only three of the seven minutes had passed. The time moved slowly, and he felt tensely coiled inside.

There hadn't been a sound from inside the large house.

The tiny numbers clicked over, past the agreed limit of four hundred and twenty seconds.

"Shit," said Kyle.

The back door was on the latch, and he eased it quietly open, finding it difficult and clumsy with the scope-sighted rifle tucked under his right arm. For a fearsome moment the tall, slender black thought he was going to drop the gun.

The smell of baking bread was stronger, flooding his nostrils, making his mouth water with a sudden hunger.

He could hear voices coming from beyond the half-closed kitchen door. But they were too faint for Kyle to pick out any words.

He edged closer, Mannlicher at his hip, finger lightly on the trigger.

Now he could make out voices. A woman, shrill and angry. A man, speaking more slowly, but overlaid with a ferocious tension. And Steve Romero, quieter and more controlled.

"I knew you'd try this, Steve."

"Why not? My boy and..." The words trailed off into something Kyle couldn't catch.

The other man's voice rose, ragged with uncontrollable anger.

"You seen the signs, Romero! We got a lot of good friends here in Aspen. We run it like always. Tight and clean and no room for outsiders. Might be a lot of folks died with Earthblood, still, around a hundred or more left and we all know each other. Look after each other."

Kyle heard Steve trying to interrupt the threatening diatribe, saying something about their not needing Sly to stay with them.

"Don't fucking need the boy! Not the point. He's big and strong and willing. New world's going to need folks like him. Doesn't matter a damn to me about the rest."

The woman spoke up. Alison. "He can tackle simple..." The rest was drowned out by her husband.

"That doesn't matter. You come here with a gun and threaten us. You won't get ten yards from Aspen once I warn the others. Track you easy in this snow. Fucking radio operator! You don't have the balls to pull the trigger.''

There was a scream and the sound of a blow, fist against flesh. Then the boom of the scattergun and another scream, much louder.

Kyle kicked the door open and burst into the living room.

33

"A hard time we had of it," said Angel McGill.

"Times we thought we wouldn't pull through," agreed Jeanne.

"Times we nearly didn't. I think that it was the children made the difference." Angel smiled and patted Jeanne on the arm. "Paul and John were just amazing, weren't they?" A brief pause. "And Pamela, as well."

Mac nodded. "Figured they'd come good. What about all the guns?"

Jeanne shook her head. "First things first, honey. Start of it all was the news bulletins about Earthblood, making it like it wasn't anything serious. But the first food shortages started almost immediately. Eggs and milk and meat."

Angel took up the story. "Phones worked then. Before the government cut them all off to stop rumors." She laughed bitterly. "Rumors! Truths is what they were. I called Jeanne up and we had a kind of coded talk. Agreed that she'd run for it, out here, with her three kids. It was the time for action."

"Got the four-by and packed everything we could inside it. Every scrap of food and tools and clothes. Left Mount Vernon Street at three in the morning. Out of Boston in twenty minutes. Got here before dawn and never regretted it for a moment."

Mac put down the empty glass. "From everything I've seen I'd say you made the right move. The big cities are overloaded with the dead. Highways blocked for miles."

"Soon as they got here, we held a council of war. Because that's what it is, Mac."

"I know it."

"Paul suggested we go down to Nevada and wait for you to land. But it was too far ahead. So John felt we should do what we could right there and then." Jeanne grinned. "That was when we formed ourselves into the McGill gang."

"Hit both gun stores in town. Course, by then, things were getting antsy. Not a spot of green to be seen. Just the sickly pinkish red color. Lot of folks were talking moving and survival.''

"We got there firstest with the mostest." Angel laughed. "Should've seen the look on old Frank Clanton's face when we all streamed in and took half his stock of weapons.''

"What did you get?" Mac rubbed his still-numbed fingers together.

"You name it we got it," Jeanne said. "Rifles, scoped and night scoped. Shotguns. Twenty-five handguns and around ten thousand rounds of assorted ammunition for them. Knives and axes. Machine pistols. And one or two other specials.''

Angel continued. "Then we hit the camping store in Hartford. Tents and sleeping bags. Armed to the teeth, we were. Desperadoes. Cooking stoves and every cylinder of gas in the place.''

"Why did you raid the two gun stores so close to home?" Mac was puzzled. "Wasn't that kind of dangerous to do?"

Angel patted him on the arm. "You were snoring away in space, lover. Society was kind of crumbling, you might say. Neither Clanton nor the police nor nobody was coming up after the mad McGills. Not when they know that we got ourselves more guns than the whole National Guard. By then the law enforcement didn't give too much of a damn."

"And Paul suggested it'd be good to let locals know just how prepared we were, so when the going got seriously tough they might leave us alone."

"That work?" he asked.

The smiles vanished. It was Angel who eventually answered him. "There's been a fair bit of killing, Mac. Mostly strangers. A few that... Shit, they were friends. Wouldn't take 'no' for an answer. We decided right at the onset that we couldn't afford to make any exceptions."

"Not one," agreed Jeanne. "Christ, but it was hard. Killing folks you'd known all your lives. But we did it."

"And you're all alive. Good wood for the winter? Gasoline? Transport? Food?"

John appeared in the doorway, a tall, powerful figure. "The McGill gang raided all over Connecticut. Biggest thing since the James and Younger boys. We worked hard,

Dad, turning the house into a fortress. Steel doors and bars and shutters."

Mac stood and embraced his oldest son. "You've done...done fucking wonderful. All of you. I can't believe you're all alive."

"What now, Mac?" asked Angel.

In the next hour or so, all of the children, with the exception of little Sukie, came into the warm room, attracted by the hum of conversation.

Mac went again through all he knew about Operation Tempest, General Zelig and the meeting in Calico in four weeks' time.

"That's all I know. I reckon there's some sort of mystery project, conjured up as a contingency plan, to counter the holocaust after Earthblood. Could be that they need specialists like me and Jim and the others."

"What happens in Calico, Dad?" asked Pamela.

"No idea."

"You noticed that there seems to be the first signs of growth coming through?" said Paul. "Winter's closing in, but by the spring..."

"Planet's healing itself after what we've done to it. Bit like an old dog shrugging off fleas. Feel fresher and better. Could be that Earth'll be like that after this winter." Mac looked around at his extended family. "By God, but I'm so proud of all of you."

Once he'd started crying, he found that he couldn't stop. He was reacting to the accumulated shocks, the fears, the grim things he'd seen and the relief.

By midnight the smaller children had been shooed off to their beds. Mac had recovered his self-control after the catharsis of weeping. He lay on the Navaho rug in front of the dying fire, while Jeanne and Angel sat on either side of the hearth.

It was his first wife who broke the comfortable silence. "So, when are you leaving for Calico?"

Mac looked around the room, pausing before he answered. "I'm not. Least, not until after the snows. April? This is where I belong. Here, with my family."

34

Ramon Hernandez hung on tenaciously to life. His spirit wanted to let go and find release, but his wiry frame clung on, the vital spark still smoldering in the shrunken, starved body.

The moment his lost daughter Heather had appeared out of the morning mists, Jim Hilton had decided to remain in his old home on Tahoe Drive, overlooking what used to be Los Angeles, until Ramon finally let go. Carrie Princip was perfectly happy to go along with his decision.

"Still plenty of time to get down to Calico, if we're still going there."

"Oh, yeah. We're still going there. All three of us."

It seemed gruesome, marking time and waiting for Ramon to die, but at least Jim was getting reacquainted with his daughter.

Relations between them were edgy at first. A gap of over two years lay between them, as did the deaths of Lori and Andrea.

The girl wouldn't talk about the cholera or about the time of Earthblood. She'd sit in the room she'd shared with her twin, until fading light forced her out into the room with the fire.

Jim noticed that she'd reverted to the books she'd read as a little girl, the old, old books by Scarry and Seuss.

Several times he'd tapped on the door and walked in, finding Heather stretched out on her bed, hands behind her head, staring blankly at the ceiling.

It was only the morning after Ramon's eventual quiet passing, when the old man had been buried alongside the other two mounds of earth, that Heather finally came out of her shell.

She joined Jim Hilton as he sat near the boundary fence, gazing out over the dull mirror of the reservoir. The light breeze was ruffling his thinning blond hair, tugging at the short sleeves of his faded maroon sports shirt.

"Can I talk, Daddy?"

"Of course. Sure you want to?"

"Think so."

Jim saw Carrie appear out of the house and start toward them. He waved a warning hand, unseen by his daughter, and the second navigator turned silently on her heel and vanished back into the shadows of the living room.

"I'm sorry I wasn't there, kitten."

She was dry-eyed, looking past him toward the rectangular blocks of the Hollywood sign. "Not your fault, Daddy."

"I was here at the end, for Andrea."

"I know, Carrie told me."

"You like her?"

The girl considered the question for a moment. "You her lover?"

"No!" he exclaimed, shocked.

For the first time since her return, Heather smiled. "Guess you're too old for her, Daddy."

"I'm not too old for... That's not the damn point, young lady, and..."

She laughed, turning her head to look into his face. "I know you aren't too old, Daddy. Only seven years older than Carrie is. That's not very much, is it? But I think she really likes you. And I mean *really* likes you."

"Heather!"

"Sorry, Daddy. Only teasing." Her eyes narrowed. "You've lost some weight. Guess everyone has since Earthblood came."

"Weighed myself in the bathroom. Down to about one-seventy. Amazing what time away from chocolate fudge does."

Her hand eased out and touched his, and his fingers tightened around hers.

"Don't look at me while I tell you, Daddy. Please. Promise?"

"Sure, kitten. I promise. And you really, truly, don't have to tell me a thing. I know what life's been like."

"No, you don't. That's the point. You *don't* know at all...."

THE SHORTAGE OF FOOD.

The government control over the television and phone systems.

Starvation riots and the trekkers coming out into the Hollywood Hills. Armed bands of hired guns patrolling the canyons, ready to mercilessly shoot down anyone attempting to get at the houses of the rich and privileged.

Power going down. And the total lack of any communication.

Driving to the reservoir to carry up water. Trying to fill their swimming pool but finding that it wouldn't stay fresh.

"Mom got sick. We'd heard about sickness from neighbors along the road. Cholera and typhoid. Ramon came around but then Maria died. We had a couple of handguns ready in case there were street thugs coming out into the hills."

"You have to use them?"

"Ramon fired once at three men in camouflage jackets. Didn't hit any of them. You killed anyone since you landed, Daddy?"

Jim Hilton shook his head. "Not something I want to talk about, kitten."

Heather still wouldn't look at her father as she sat cross-legged on the dead grass, voice flat and unemotional.

"Mom got worse. Then . . . sissy got it."

That had been the twins' nickname for each other when they'd been smaller.

Lori Hilton had died from cholera, a dreadful sickness when there are no doctors and no kind of medication. Not even clean water.

It had been Andrea's rapid decline that had proved the final straw for Heather.

"The way Mommy went was...and I knew that Andrea would be the same. I kind of starred out in my head. Just ran. I was away for three or four days. Lost count. Slept rough. Came back to see if she was still alive. And found you...burying her. Couldn't believe it, that you'd come back."

He hugged her tightly. "Take more than the end of life on the planet as we know it to keep me away from you, kitten."

JIM HAD BEEN pleasantly surprised at how his daughter was coping. It gave him an insight into the horrors of life under Earthblood, the strength growing out of such extreme circumstances enabling a child of eleven to witness deaths, including her own mother, and still be able to function.

Carrie spoke to him that evening about it.

"Kids are resilient, Jim. In the old days I suppose that Heather would have been rushed off to a fashionable shrink, for some infinitely tiny problem. I'm not saying it's easy for the kid. But she can take it." She hesitated. "You think you can, Jim?"

"Reckon so."

"We going to take her back to this ghost town with us?"

"Course. Why not?"

"Wondered if you might want to stay here and try and...you know, make some sort of life together. Just wondered."

"No, Carrie. City's no place now. Probably never will be again. Life has to be radically different. It's almost like going back to the Middle Ages. Little villages. If the plants and trees really start to grow again, next year, then there's a chance."

"And Zelig?"

He smiled. "Zelig! Who knows. Just got to go and find out. We'll take it easy. Weather's getting worse, so we can't go into the hills too much. Get back to Calico and see who else turns up there."

IN HOLLYWOOD, even the early days of November are mild and clement. Jim went out in the evenings among the budding shoots of grass and killed rabbits with the big .44, its boom contrasting with the snap of Carrie's Smith & Wesson six-shot .22 revolver.

Eventually it was time to set off for Calico.

They all stood together in the front garden of the house on Tahoe Drive in the cool morning air.

"Ready, kitten?" said Jim.

His daughter half turned to Carrie, eyebrows raised, chin tilted in a way that reminded him of Lori.

"I wish Daddy wouldn't call me 'kitten,'" she said.

35

It was a standoff.

Kyle stood in the doorway, the Model V Mannlicher rifle braced against his right hip, finger on the trigger. He was trying to remember whether he'd taken off the safety, mentally cursing himself for his stupidity.

The woman standing near the fireplace in the living room didn't look stupid, and she was holding a blue-steel automatic as if she *knew* the safety was off.

Kyle figured that this must be Alison, Steve Romero's wife.

There was a huge man, with a crew cut so severe that his skull burst out through it. He was wearing stained blue chinos and a faded sweatshirt that gaped over his belly.

That had to be Randy.

Steve Romero was backed against the wall, holding the smoking sawed-down 12 gauge. A pitted hole on the far wall, close by the window, showed where his shot had gone wide. Kyle noticed that his friend had a darkening bruise on his cheekbone and a thread of blood creeping down his chin from the corner of his mouth.

A lamp had been knocked over, spilling pungent oil across the wooden floor. Another stood near the door, its golden glow leaving the room in pools of light and shadow.

Kyle noticed a fourth person standing behind the woman, but he was mainly in darkness. He figured that this must be Sly, Steve's eighteen-year-old son. The boy completely motionless, hands clenched at his sides.

"This the nigger cavalry?" said Randy slowly, grinning at Kyle.

"Who you going to shoot with that deer rifle, boy?" sneered the woman. "Bolt action like that, you'll only get off one shot. Then either I shoot you in the guts or Randy rips off your balls and stuffs them down you throat."

"I'll wipe you away, bitch," growled Steve, gesturing with the shotgun.

"Not unless you put another shell into that little shotgun," said Randy.

Kyle found that his brain had turned to frozen Jell-O. There were so many permutations that he couldn't make any sort of decision. It seemed that he had to try to shoot someone, but the woman was the most likely target. It didn't seem easy to pull the trigger.

The barrel of the Mannlicher wavered indecisively between Alison and the hulking Randy.

"You boys just walk outside and keep walking and never come back," suggested the woman. She had the faded prettiness of a once-good-looking woman who now enjoyed her liquor.

"Yeah. Get the fuck out," ehoed Randy.

"I've come for Sly. Come for my son. I want to take him with me to somewhere better than this." Steve's voice was surprisingly steady.

"No fucking way. Sly's real useful here."

"Sure. Useful. But you don't love him. You never have."

Alison laughed, a hard sound like brittle steel. "Course. I don't think anyone could love *that*," she said, gesturing behind her with the small pistol.

"I love him and I want him. Won't leave without him."

"Then there'll be blood on the floor. The nigger with the rifle first, and then you."

"Shoot her, Kyle," said Steve. "Come on, man, just do it."

"I'm going to... going..." But his heart told him he wasn't.

It was the large figure of the boy in the shadows that broke the moment of paralysis.

He loomed up behind his mother and clubbed her clumsily across the back of the head with the flat of his hand.

"You won't hurt Dad," he shouted.

Alison went down like a heifer under the poleax, the gun dropping to the parquet.

Randy was quick off the mark for a big man, but he wasn't quick enough to beat the .357 Magnum round from the rifle.

It hit him in the chest, just to the right of the sternum, spinning him around and dumping him in a yelping tangle of arms and legs by the fire.

Kyle brought the Mannlicher to his shoulder, all the hesitation and fear gone. Ignoring the scope sight, he centered the barrel on Randy as he struggled to his feet, blood already staining his shirt.

The second bullet smashed through the open mouth, taking out several teeth, most of the tongue, the soft palate and a fair part of the lower brain before it exited, distorted and mangled, into the blazing logs in the hearth.

"You bastard," breathed Kyle quietly.

They dragged the heavy body outside into the blizzard and left it beyond the shelter of the rear porch.

Steve had tied up his hysterical ex-wife, bound her wrists behind her with another strong cord around her neck, knotted to the frame of the double bed in the end room.

He'd attempted to gag her, trying to stop the flood of foul and abusive language. But Steve's skill wasn't up to it, and he'd given up. He simply closed the door on her, partially muffling the screams.

Kyle was sitting by the fire, head down, trying to overcome his shakiness. He'd managed to reload the rifle.

Steve had picked up the fallen automatic, finding it was an ancient German Beholla Pocket Auto, a seven-shot, .32 caliber handgun with a stubby three-inch barrel and ribbed rubber stock.

He'd also found a couple of boxes of ammunition in a kitchen drawer and given half to Kyle to load up the empty Mondadori automatic.

Sly had thrown himself down on the sofa immediately after Randy's death and refused to move or even speak. He was a large, clumsy-looking boy, in a dark sweater and baggy jeans. Kyle still hadn't had a chance to see his face, wondering if he favored his mother or Steve.

His friend walked back into the room. "We'll stay the night and move at dawn. It's a long hard road. If the snow's still falling, we'd best wait."

Kyle nodded. "What about Alison?"

"Stays where she is. If someone comes along and finds her, then she lives. If not..." He allowed the sentence to trail away.

"Taking Sly?"

"Of course." Steve sat down and patted the boy on the back. "Sly's a part of the family now. But what about you, Kyle?"

"What?"

"Leanne in Albuquerque?"

"Oh, yeah. Well, fact is she and I were sort of breaking up before the *Aquila* blasted off. Been seeing a lady called Rosa, just now and then. No, I'll join you on the road to Calico."

SLY FELL ASLEEP, face down, breathing heavily.

Alison had become quieter, though she still shrieked out occasional threats promising them that she'd come after them and that there was some mysterious group of men who would hunt them down.

Steve had gone in to try to gag her again, leaving Kyle to stand and stare out at the steadily falling snow. A shuffling sound from behind him made Kyle turn around.

Sly was standing up, rubbing his eyes. He dropped his hands and stared curiously at Kyle.

"You're a friend of my dad's?" he said.

"Yeah."

Now that he could finally see the eighteen-year-old clearly, a lot of things made sense. Sly had a round, soft face, with a gentle, moonish smile. He also had the distinctive hooded eyes of someone with Down's syndrome.

THE SNOW DIDN'T STOP until the middle of the next morning, but the two friends agreed that they'd get moving immediately. Alison's repeated threats about the vigilante groups made them feel they wanted out of Aspen as soon as possible.

They'd stocked up their packs with what food they could find, and Steve had spent some time helping Sly to get dressed in thermal underclothes and several layers of jumpers and shirts.

The boy was excited about their journey.

"We going to meet all the other astronauts, Dad?" he'd asked.

"Yeah. Hope so, son."

They looked in on the woman before they left. But she refused to speak to them, trying to spit at her ex-husband as he turned away.

They heard her through the closed door. "You fucking wait, Steve!"

Sly decided that he had to take a last-minute pee. Waiting for him in the kitchen, Kyle and Steve looked out at the white mound that was Randy's corpse.

"Does it make any difference to you having the boy along, Kyle? The way he is, you know?"

"Yeah. The difference it makes, Steve, is that I'm even more pleased we came to Colorado to get him."

36

The days in the Jackson Street apartment drifted by in a bizarre, almost timeless world.

Nanci Simms had totally taken over the running of Jeff Thomas's life, imposing her forceful personality on him.

She refused to allow him into San Francisco, pointing out she'd already rescued him once and didn't intend to have to do it again.

Every now and again she would leave, generally just after midnight, with the Port Royale machine pistol slung over her elegant shoulders and a pair of matched Heckler & Koch P-111 automatics at her hip. Both held fifteen rounds of 9mm full-metal-jacket ammunition.

Three times Jeff woke to find her seated in his kitchen, her silver head stooped over the candle-lit table, fieldstripping her greased weapons and carefully reloading them.

She brought back food and drink, including a bottle of fine Polish vodka.

They would sit and discuss the Civil War battles for hours, using his models to play over the various elements of the long campaigns.

For much of this time, Jeff Thomas was really happy. He felt secure with her, warm and well fed, while the anarchy outside rarely intruded.

One morning he woke to hear her easing open the security door, the Port Royale in her hands. She was wearing only a white cotton T-shirt and pale purple satin bikini pants. Despite her age, Nanci's body was in fantastic condition.

Seeing him awake, she put a finger to her lips, then vanished into the corridor. Several minutes later Jeff heard the silk-ripping sound of the gun on full auto.

A couple of days before, Nanci had stolen a gun for him, a stainless-steel Smith & Wesson 4506. The big .45 had an 8-round magazine, a five-inch barrel and wraparound Delrin stocks and a serrated hammer spur with adjustable rear sight.

"It will stop a charging buffalo," she'd said. "Only advice I'll give you, Jeff, is to use it when you mean it and mean it when you use it.''

Now, with the gunfire still echoing in his ears, he grabbed it and ran out of the door, picking his way down the stairs to the second floor. He found her there calmly checking that each of the four bodies at her feet were all dead.

They were.

She looked up and saw him there, wearing only his underpants, holding the gun.

"Come here," she said. "My firm recollection is that I told you never to come out unless I called for you."

"Thought you might need help."

"Nice thought, but wrong." She slapped him so hard and fast across the face, both cheeks, that he nearly fell over. "It's important that you learn to do what I say."

"Sorry," he muttered.

Then Nanci had smiled, reached out with her right hand and slid it inside his pants to cup him with strong fingers, bringing him to instant hardness. "Nice of you to worry, though. Now let us go up to bed and make some long, slow loving."

Jeff had never made love to a woman over sixty before. In fact, as he studied himself in the full-length bathroom mirror afterward, he couldn't remember making love to any woman over twenty-one.

His face showed the marks of her slap, and his cheeks and chin were reddened from her insistence on his pleasuring her with his tongue.

There were scratches on his shoulder and across his lower stomach. His jaw ached, and much lower down it felt as though he had been massaged with a red chili paste.

But it had been the best sex he'd ever known.

THE DIGITAL calendar clock on the wall of the kitchen showed November 12, 2040, eleven-thirty at night. Outside it was a dull, cold evening, with a mixture of fog and drizzle coming in off the bay.

They'd just been reworking the Battle of Chickamauga, with its dubious, hollow triumph for the army of Tennessee. Thirty-five thousand men fallen and nothing gained.

Nanci had stood up and stretched. "Bedtime, Jefferson. Get that educated tongue of yours ready to give me some slow loving." She looked at the tiny figures in blue and gray. "Shame we have to leave in the morning. I was working up to Sherman's march to the sea."

"Can we take the models with us, Nanci?"

"No. Not enough space in the Mercedes."

"The what?"

"Found it days ago," she said, her hand resting on his shoulder and sending a thrill of pleasure through him. "Got it filled up with gas and garaged out on Cedar, near Van Ness."

"Terrific. I like to go in style."

"So you're grateful to me, Jeff?"

"Yeah."

"Good." Her fingers slid inside his shirt, over his chest, seeking the left nipple, finding it and tightening, making him gasp with pain and excitement. She squeezed tighter, making him bite his lip. Her face was against his, her breath warm on his cheek. "I trust that you'll be very grateful to me, Jeff."

"Oh, God, yes," he sighed.

NANCI INSISTED on doing all the driving herself. She pushed on fast, finding ways around what looked like impossible traffic blocks. The silver Mercedes rolled on like a dream, the soft top down in the warm sunshine. South toward Los Angeles.

"I could spell you at the wheel," he offered in midafternoon.

"This is not a casual spin out into the Sierras for transient pleasure. This is now and this is real."

Camp was set for the night near Alta Sierra, close by Isabella Lake. They weren't too far north of L.A., and on their way to closing in on Calico.

Jeff felt slightly sick from the long drive and he was relieved when Nanci didn't call on him for sexual services.

She had lit a small fire and cooked the remains of a cat she'd snared in San Francisco.

"Nanci?"

"You're going to ask me *again* about what I really used to do for a living. I'd prefer it if you didn't, Jefferson."

"You said you'd been a teacher. And a contract assassin for Central Intelligence. I believe both of them. By God, I do! But how do you know about Zelig? What's going on, Nanci?"

She turned, hair tinted crimson by the fire's glow, her eyes like burning rubies.

"It is probably a cliché, but it is honestly better for you that you don't know too much. Either you trust me or you don't. But don't ask. One day, if the lords of chaos are willing, you'll find out."

SEVENTY MILES short of Calico, beyond Mojave, Jeff saw a half-dozen figures strung out across the highway, stunted by the perspective and the shimmering desert heat.

Nanci took her foot off the gas, letting the Mercedes whisper down to something closer to fifty than ninety.

"They might be..." he began.

"Shut up and grab hold of that .45, there's a good boy."

The figures were closer, taking individual shapes. Dark blue pants, peaked caps with silver badges, polished mirror sunglasses that concealed the eyes. Four in leather jackets, the other two in shirtsleeves. All of them were holding drawn revolvers that glittered in the morning sunlight.

"Fucking cops," said Jeff.

"Ten out of ten for surface observation. Zero out of ten for intelligence."

"You mean they aren't—"

He was pushed back in the bucket seat as the Mercedes suddenly accelerated hard toward the line of men.

Jeff had a splinter of a frozen second to wonder if this was where he became dead.

37

Captain James Hilton, lately the commander of the United States Space Vessel *Aquila*, stared down the sunlit main street of the ghost town.

There was the dazzle of the chromed hood of the sleek silver Mercedes sports car parked near the open front of what had once been a gift shop. Wind chimes still tinkled in the light breeze, and you could just taste the faint, elusive flavor of piñon pine candles.

There were five bullet holes in the car, not counting the smashed windshield. The front fender was crumpled and smeared with gobbets of brown, drying blood. One of the double headlights was gone, and Jim could still make out the macabre hank of blond-haired scalp that dangled from the socket.

He'd personally removed the severed finger from the radiator grill, noticing that the sterling silver ring was monogrammed C.H.P.

The rough surface of the old picnic table in front of him felt warm to the touch. Jim glanced at the sky, seeing it cloudless from east to west.

It was 15 November 2040.

The date and the place that Zelig had warned them to attend.

He looked around, seeing what changes the past seven eventful weeks had wrought in his command. Mentally he ticked off the names. Finding, to his dismay, that some of the faces had blurred.

Bob Rogers from Topeka, dead in his cryo-capsule.

Mike Man, the best chess player that Jim had ever known, dead in the landing crash.

Marcey Cortling, the *Aquila*'s number two, decapitated.

Ryan O'Keefe, their psychiatrist, also dead at Stevenson base.

Jed Herne, shot by a sniper, not far from San Francisco, his death described to them by Jeff Thomas that morning.

Pete Turner and Henderson McGill, both missing. Believed killed. Their planned trip up to New England was the longest and the most dangerous. Mac's loss was about the hardest of the crew to bear.

Seven dead or lost, and the survivors from the *Aquila*.

Himself.

Steve Romero and Kyle Lynch, going out together and returning together.

Jeff Thomas, beating the odds to return to Calico.

And Carrie, who'd been such a vital support for Jim through the past seven weeks.

Seven from twelve.

But they also had some additions.

His own daughter, Heather, sitting on the porch of what used to be the house of the town's schoolteacher. She was playing a game with a handful of quartz pebbles with ever-smiling Sly Romero.

Jim turned his head to the north, where the ground rose steeply, close by the remains of an old mining railway. He'd felt the woman's presence before he saw her, conscious of the intensity of her gaze.

The enigmatic Nanci Simms, immaculate in her khaki trouser suit and polished boots, was standing on the ridge and staring at him.

There were some questions there, but they could wait awhile.

There was no sign of Zelig. No sign of anyone moving for as far as the eye could see. Just the ocher expanse of the desert, stretching away, unchanged and eternal.

Jim sighed. "What now?" he said.

Take
4 explosive books
plus a
mystery bonus
FREE

Are you looking for more

DEATHLANDS®
by James Axler

Don't miss these stories by one of Gold Eagle's most
popular authors:

GOLD EAGLE ®